BEND IT
LIKE BECKHAM

D0995868

Other  titles

BEND IT
LIKE BECKHAM

NARINDER DHAMI

Based on the original screenplay by Gurinder Chadha,
Guljit Bindra and Paul Mayeda Berges

**Hodder
Children's
Books**

a division of Hodder Headline Limited

Script copyright © 2002 Bilb Productions Limited
Novelisation copyright © 2002 Narinder Dhami

First published in Great Britain in 2002
by Hodder Children's Books

The right of Narinder Dhami to be identified as the
Author of this Work has been asserted by her in accordance
with the Copyright, Designs and Patents Act 1988.

10 9 8 7 6 5 4

A Catalogue record for this book is available from
the British Library

ISBN 0 340 86094 4

Typeset by Avon Dataset Ltd, Bidford-on-Avon, Warks

Printed and bound in Great Britain by
Bookmarque Ltd, Croydon, Surrey

The paper and board used in this paperback by Hodder
Children's Books are natural recyclable products made from wood grown in
sustainable forests. The manufacturing processes
conform to the enviromental regulations of the country of origin.

Hodder Children's Books
a division of Hodder Headline Ltd
338 Euston Road
London NW1 3BH

ONE

Old Trafford. Manchester United v. Anderlecht. The crowd a sea of red and white. They're on edge, waiting for the all-important goal.

'But there's a big question mark hanging over Manchester United,' John Motson says breathlessly. 'Where's the goal going to come from? Will it be Scholes? Could it be Ryan Giggs? Or will David Beckham himself break through?'

The crowd lean forward, urging the players on. The atmosphere is electric.

'Oh, and there's the ball Beckham wanted! Plenty of players in the middle, and Bhamra's making ground as well. It's a decent cross, and there's Bhamra. That's a fine header – AND SHE SCORES!'

The crowd go wild.

'And it's a goal by Jess Bhamra! A superb header, beating the defender and planting the ball just out of reach past the goalkeeper. Jess Bhamra makes a name for herself at Old Trafford! Have we discovered a new star here, Gary?'

Back in the TV studios, Gary Lineker turns to

Alan Hansen and John Barnes. They all look well impressed.

'Good question, Motty,' says Gary, turning to the panel. '*Could* Jess Bhamra be the answer to England's prayers, Alan?'

Alan raises his eyebrows. 'There's no denying the talent there, Gary. She's quick-thinking, comfortable on the ball, she's got awareness and vision. I tell you what, I wish she was playing for Scotland.'

Gary laughs and turns to John Barnes. 'John, do you think England have found the player to help them relive our 1966 World Cup glory?'

'No question, Gary,' says John. 'I think we've finally got the missing piece of the jigsaw. And, the best thing is, she's not even reached her peak yet.'

Gary turns to the camera. 'Now, joining us in the studio is Jess's mother, Mrs Bhamra.'

MUM?! Get out of my fantasy!

'So, Mrs Bhamra, you must be very proud of your daughter?' Gary beams.

'Not at all!' shrieks Mum. 'She shouldn't be running around with all these men, showing her bare legs to seventy thousand people. She's bringing shame on her family –' she gives the panel a filthy look '– and you three shouldn't be encouraging her.'

Gary, Alan and John look like little boys who've just been told off by their teacher.

'Jesminder, you get back home right now!' Mum rants on, pointing her finger at the camera. 'Wait till I get hold of you! Jesminder . . .'

A second later, my bedroom door crashed open.

'Jesminder, are you listening to me?' Mum demanded.

Why did she always have to interrupt at the best bits? Gary was about to interview Sven-Goran Eriksson, who was considering calling me up for the next England match.

'Jesminder, have you gone mad?' Mum pointed at the TV and glared at me. Her special *Listen to me, I'm your mother and I know best* glare. 'Football shootball! It's your sister's engagement party tomorrow, and you're sitting here watching that skinhead boy.'

She grabbed the remote control from me, and snapped the TV off. I groaned.

'Oh, *Mum*, it's Beckham's corner.'

Mum took no notice. She never does. 'Come downstairs,' she ordered me. 'Your sister's going crazy.'

Tell me something I don't know. Pinky's pretty

crazy, anyway. Now, with her wedding coming up, she's a full-on lunatic. I could hear her downstairs right now, having a fit about something or other.

I stood up with a sigh. My bedroom was the only place I could really chill out, but even here I couldn't get any peace and quiet half the time. I had the room exactly how I wanted it, even though Mum never stopped moaning. Pictures of David Beckham everywhere, and my Manchester United Number 7 shirt hanging on the wall. Beckham was my hero. OK, I know what you're thinking. Yes, he's gorgeous. You'd have to be blind not to see it. But that's not why I like him. He's a god on the football pitch. *No-one* can bend a ball like Beckham.

'I'm sick of this wedding, and it hasn't even started yet,' I muttered, staring at the poster of Becks over my bed. I talked to him all the time.

Beckham looked back at me as if he understood. He always understood. Nobody else did. Not in this house, anyway. It was just 'football shootball'. I remembered a quote by a famous Liverpool manager that I'd read the other day. *Some people think football's a matter of life and death. It's much more important than that.* That was exactly how I felt.

I went downstairs as slowly as I could. Pinky was

standing in the hall, looking like she was about to rip someone's head off with her bare hands.

'Why else would she do this at the last minute?' she was screaming. 'She wants to ruin it for me. I'm telling you, Mum, she's a first-class bitch.'

'Pinky!' Mum scolded, rushing down the stairs and into the kitchen. 'You've got plenty of others.'

'But it's all *planned*,' Pinky wailed. 'I need another one now.' She shot me a poisonous stare. 'Will you get a flaming move on!'

'What's going on?' I asked. It sounded as if someone had died, at the very least.

Pinky turned on me. 'Get this. Teet's bloody sister's gone and said *she's* wearing baby pink to our engagement party now.' If looks could kill, her fiance's sister would have dropped down dead on the spot. 'And I've got all my matching accessories and *everything*.'

I nearly said Is *that all?*, but luckily stopped myself just in time. Or it would have been *me* lying dead in the hall. 'Oh, Mum,' I groaned. 'Do I have to go shopping AGAIN?'

Mum charged out of the kitchen, shaking a carrot at me. 'My mother chose all my twenty-one dowry suits herself – and I never complained once. You girls are too spoiled.' She waved us out of the door. 'And don't forget my *dhania*. Four bunches for a pound. Oh, and some more carrots.'

This wedding was getting well out of hand, I thought, clinging to the dashboard as Pinky drove like a maniac to Southall Broadway. And we still had to get through the engagement ceremony tomorrow night first.

'We'll go to Damini's,' Pinky ordered, breezing along the Broadway like she owned it. She'd taken her denim jacket off, and in her skimpy red top, sprayed-on jeans and sunglasses, she was turning a lot of guys' heads. No-one was looking at me in my Adidas sweatpants and top. But that was the way I liked it.

My sister's the shopper from hell. We spent an hour in Daminis looking at suits. We didn't buy any of them. Then she dragged me into Ajanta Footwear to look at shoes. I didn't bother pointing out that it wasn't worth looking at shoes until we'd bought the suit. The mood Pinky was in, she'd probably have thrown me under a bus just for mentioning it.

'Oh no,' I heard Pinky mutter as we went into the shop.

Our cousins, Meena, Bubbly and Monica, were in Ajanta, trying on shoes. They're all right, I guess. If you like bubble-headed bimbos with only two things on their mind – boys and clothes. They were all wearing strappy little tops and tight jeans, and they had dyed hair with streaky highlights. They think they're the Indian version of Jennifer Aniston. They wish. I saw Pinky's face drop, then she put on this really fake smile and rushed over to them like she hadn't seen them for five years.

'Hi! *Mwah! Mwah!*'

There was a lot of hugging and air-kissing going on. I just stuck my hands in the pockets of my sweatpants, and tried to look invisible.

'Whatcha doin' here, man?' squealed Monica. 'You haven't left everything till the last minute, have you?'

Pinky laughed. 'Yeah, one more day of freedom!'

Monica, Bubbly and Meena laughed too, but they all looked a bit sick. They were probably wishing it was *them* getting married.

My heart sank as I saw Pinky suddenly stare Monica straight in the eye. 'When did you get your contacts?' she asked in a frosty voice.

Oh no, I thought.

Monica looked smug. 'D'ya like them? I just thought they went with my hair.'

'Oh.' Pinky went in for the kill. 'My fiancé doesn't like dyed hair.' She smirked as Monica looked furious. 'Still, can't stand here chatting all day. I'm going to Ealing for my facial. Laters.'

'Bye, Pinky, laters,' the three airheads chorused.

Pinky grabbed my arm and pulled me over to the door. 'Stupid bitch,' she moaned in my ear. 'Why'd she have to go and get blue contacts? Now I can't wear mine!'

I had to bite my tongue to keep quiet. We'd be shopping for new body parts next.

'I might go back to Daminis,' Pinky went on as we carried on along the Broadway. 'I really liked that lace lycra outfit.' Then she nudged me. 'Look, Jess, there's your mate.'

Tony was coming towards us with his mum, his arms full of shopping. Don't get the wrong idea about Tony. I've known him for years, and I like him a lot. But not like *that*.

'Let's make this quick,' Pinky hissed in my ear. She glared at Tony's mum, who was shuffling along behind him, peering through her thick glasses, her scarf wrapped round her head. 'And I hope your mate's mum wears a cardi over her three stomachs at the party tomorrow.'

'Shut up, she's old,' I muttered.

'So?' Pinky shot back.

Tony looked shyly at us. That doesn't *mean* anything, though. He was just embarrassed at being caught with his mum, carrying a big bag of onions and a family pack of loo roll. 'Hiya, Jess. Hi, Pinky.'

'Saat Sri Akal, Massiji,' Pinky and I said, putting our hands together.

Tony's mum beamed at us. 'May you have a long life, my daughters. Everything ready for tomorrow?'

'Yes, Massiji,' Pinky replied, doing her good little Indian girl act. 'Mum's making the samosas.'

'May God keep you and your husband in endless happiness!' Tony's mum said loudly. I'm not kidding, she really does talk like that. 'And pray for me, so that I get a good daughter-in-law like you for my Tony, eh, *beta*?'

I couldn't help grinning at Tony, who looked like he wanted to jump down the nearest hole.

'Thank you, Massiji,' Pinky said quickly. I could tell she was dying to get away. 'OK, bye . . .'

'How was biology?' Tony jumped in, just before Pinky could drag me away.

We'd just done our A-levels, and Tony and I had revised together – in-between football games!

'OK,' I said. 'Did you do the genetics question?'

Tony nodded, and we compared notes on our answers. Luckily we'd put down the same.

'Hope I get my two As and a B for uni,' I said, sighing. Mum and Dad had plans for me to become a solicitor after I got my A-level results next month. I hadn't objected so far because I didn't really know *what* I wanted to do. Except play football. And that wasn't a proper job. Not for a girl, anyway.

'Come *on*, Jess,' Pinky breathed impatiently in my ear.

'You going to the park later, Jess?' Tony asked hopefully. What he really meant was, Are you up for a game of footie later with the lads?

'I'll try,' I said. A kick-around was just what I needed to forget all about the wedding for a few hours. 'Saat Sri Akal, Massiji.'

I waved to Tony and his mum. As they went off, Pinky gave a shriek of joy which could probably be heard all the way over in Hounslow.

'I've found it!' She pointed in the window of the nearest sari shop at a lilac and cerise suit. 'Come on, Jess!'

Thank God, I said silently, as she dragged me inside.

The next major trauma was when we got back to the car, and remembered that we'd forgotten the *dhania* and the carrots for Mum. Pinky didn't want to be late for her facial, so she dropped me off and I bought the stuff at Gill's Mini-market. I walked home from there, and decided to take a short cut through the park. It really *is* a short cut. Honest.

Tony and some of the boys – Taz, Sonny, Gary and a couple of others – were in the middle of a game. Swinging the carrier bag full of coriander and carrots, I slowed down to watch.

Tony saw me, and his face lit up. He came running over. 'Hey, Jess, fancy a quick game?'

'I can't,' I said reluctantly. 'My mum's waiting, and my dad's on earlies at Heathrow.'

'Aw, come on, Jess,' Tony pleaded. 'We really need you.'

I hesitated.

'Come *on*.' Tony grabbed my arm.

I dropped the carrier bag on a nearby bench, and ran over to join the others. Taz and Sonny started whistling and yelling stuff, but they're always like that, so I took no notice. They're OK really. Just more brawn than brains.

The game started up again, and within seconds I had the ball. Sonny ran at me, but I could see him coming a mile off. I sidestepped him easily, and headed for goal. Out of the corner of my eye, I spotted Taz heading towards me. I stopped the ball suddenly, did a double step over it, completely wrong-footed him and left him for dead. I couldn't understand why my brain seemed to work a hundred times faster when I was playing football. I just loved the fact that it did.

Looking frustrated, Taz lunged at me again from the side. He slid in and took my ankles from underneath me. Free kick.

'Does she think she's Beckham or what?' Gary grumbled. Forget sexual equality. Boys still *hate* being beaten by girls.

'Yeah, can you chest it like him, Jess?' Sonny sniggered, grabbing his bare chest. None of the boys were wearing shirts. 'Y'know, give it some *bounce*?'

Taz grabbed his own chest, pretending he had boobs. 'Go on, Jess, chest it!'

I flicked the ball into the air with my heels, caught it, strolled over to them and pushed it into Taz's nuts. He yelled in pain and doubled over, and the other boys fell about laughing. Smiling to myself, I grabbed the carrier bag, and headed for home.

'It's not fair.' I lay with my head at the foot of my bed, staring up at Beckham. 'I could've carried on playing all night. The boys never have to come home and help . . .'

I'd run all the way home, but Mum had still complained that I'd been too long. She'd taken one look at my muddy trainers, and guessed I'd been playing football in the park too. That always put her in a bad mood.

'I wonder,' I went on thoughtfully, 'if I had an arranged marriage, would I get someone who'd let me play football whenever I wanted?'

The door opened, and I jumped.

'*Putar*, who are you talking to?' my dad asked, looking puzzled. He'd just got back from work, and he was still in his security guard's uniform.

'No-one,' I said quickly.

Dad came in and sat down on the bed. 'You know Biji and her grandson will be staying in here when they arrive for the wedding.' He stared around the room. '*Putar*, why don't you put up some nice pictures of beautiful scenery instead of this bald man?'

'Dad!' I groaned.

He smiled at me and stroked my hair. 'OK, I'm going to change. Then come and help me outside.'

I rolled off the bed. We had a whole load of fairy lights to put on the outside of the house, ready for the engagement party, and I bet Mum had plenty of last-minute jobs lined up for me too. No chance of a game tomorrow then . . .

To be honest, the engagement party wasn't *that* bad. The house looked fantastic with all the lights shimmering in the dark, and there was enough food to feed the whole of Southall. All the relatives had turned out, and the living-room was packed with people. The men were in suits and ties, including Tony, and the women were dressed up like Christmas trees. Monica, Bubbly and Meena were there, eyeing up all the girls' outfits and deciding how much they'd cost. I bet they didn't spend very long discussing *mine*. My blue shalwaar kameez was the plainest Mum would let me get away with.

Pinky looked nervous but happy as she sat next to Teetu, playing the part of the quiet, shy bride-to-be.

She'd been seeing Teets for years, even going behind Mum and Dad's back at first. He was nice enough, but a bit of a wheeler dealer. I didn't really have a clue what Pinky saw in him, but she was mad about the guy.

None of us were mad about his family, though. His sister was looking so smug in her baby pink, that I was a bit worried Pinky would get up and punch her on the nose. And Teetu's mum was scary. I was being a good, helpful daughter, carrying round a large plate of Indian sweets, and I offered it to them. Teetu's dad went to take one, and she actually slapped his hand and told him off. I didn't envy Pinky having that miserable old bag for a mother-in-law.

There was a long row of beady-eyed aunties sitting on the sofa, watching everything that was going on. I took the sweets over to them, fixing a smile on my face.

'It'll be your turn soon, Jesminder,' one of them said gleefully. 'Do you want a clean-shaven boy like your sister, or a proper Sikh with full beard and turban?'

I didn't want to answer that. Not that I'd even thought about it. *I don't want to get married*, I said silently. Not until I've done something with my life, anyway. I didn't want what Pinky wanted. I was looking for something different, although I didn't know what. And anyway, there was more to life than getting married.

Like football, for instance.

TWO

'Oh, yes!' I ran across the grass, punching the air with my fist. 'What a goal!'

I'd just scored with a hard, right-footed shot that had blasted its way past the goalie. Taz and Gary looked well fed up. They glared at each other, as Tony and I celebrated.

'Hey, man, what were you waiting for?' Gary roared at Taz. 'A flippin' bus?'

I grinned to myself as Taz took his shirt off and threw it down on the ground in disgust.

'Oi, Jess! Over here!'

I looked round. Monica, Bubbly and Meena were sitting on a nearby bench, waving frantically at me.

'What do *they* want?' I thought irritably. They didn't bother with me much, usually. Reluctantly I ran over to them. They were all tarted up as usual, and were completely overdressed for sitting in the park. But then, they didn't look too impressed with my Manchester United shirt and trackies either.

'Jess, man, who's your friend with the gorgeous bod?' Monica demanded.

'Who?' I didn't have a clue what they were talking about.

'The one with the six-pack,' Meena squealed impatiently.

'If he looks at me, I really will faint,' Monica said in this totally melodramatic voice.

I frowned and looked over at the boys. 'Do you mean Taz?'

'Taz, is that his name?' Monica asked eagerly. Their tongues were practically hanging out as they watched Taz fooling around, doing stupid kung-fu moves on the other lads. 'He is so *fine*.'

'Hey, Jess,' Tony called to me. 'Come on.'

Thank God. I'd had enough of all this girly stuff.

'Go on, Jess,' Bubbly said cattily. 'Lover boy's calling you.'

'Shut up,' I snapped. 'You know he's just my mate. We're not all slags like you lot.'

I turned and ran off, feeling really annoyed. I didn't want anyone getting the wrong idea about me and Tony. Auntie's words came flooding back: *It'll be your turn soon* . . . Not likely! I shook my head and jogged back on to the pitch.

Taz and Gary were determined to stop me this time, but when Tony passed me the ball, I took them on again. I wrong-footed Taz. Then I pushed the ball past Gary, ran round him and collected it on the other side. It was just too easy. Before they knew what had hit them, I'd scored again. Taz and Gary were so mad, I thought they were going to kill each other.

We were walking back to restart the game, when I saw a girl coming towards us. At first I didn't take any notice, thinking that she was just using the pitch as a short cut. But she was looking straight at me and smiling.

'Hi.'

'Er – hi.' I stared at her. She was tall and thin, with short blonde hair, and she was wearing a trackie top and shorts. She was pretty too. But I'd never seen her before in my life.

'That was brilliant,' she said eagerly. 'Do you play for any side?'

I was completely gobsmacked. I glanced at Tony, who looked puzzled too. The other lads nearly bust a gut laughing. Typical.

'Like who?' Taz grinned. 'Southall United Sari Squad?'

The girl ignored him. She obviously wasn't as impressed with Taz's six-pack as Meena, Monica and Bubbly were. 'I play for Hounslow Harriers girls' side.' I looked blank. I didn't know there *was* a Hounslow Harriers girls' side. 'It's closed season now, but we've got a summer tournament coming up.' She smiled at me. 'You should come and have a trial.'

'A trial?' I stammered. I couldn't get my head round what she was saying. 'Do you think I'm good enough?'

The girl nodded. 'Yeah. I've watched you a few times while I've been out running. You've got really good. It's up to our coach, but –' she shrugged '– I know we could do with some fresh blood.'

'That's brilliant, Jess,' Tony said excitedly.

The boys started laughing hysterically again.

'Nice one, Jess,' Taz teased. 'D'ya swap shirts at the end of matches?'

'And get in the big bath together?' Sonny added.

The girl raised her eyebrows at me and shook her head. 'I'm Jules,' she said, stretching out a hand.

'Jess,' I said breathlessly. I didn't care how much the boys laughed at me. Jules thought I was good enough to play for a *proper* side. At last, this was my chance to do something different with my life. *This* was what I'd been waiting for.

* * *

I stood at the side of the pitch, trying to take it all in. Hounslow Harriers had a *real* ground. A proper pitch with lights and corner flags and changing-rooms and stands for the crowd. Instead of Taz and Sonny and Gary and the others taking the mick and fooling about, there were women doing some serious training on the pitch in front of me. They were all different. Some of them were slim and lean, like Jules, and some of them were more powerfully-built, like athletes. There were a couple of black girls, but no Indians. No surprise there, then.

My heart thumped with excitement. Those were the girls I'd be playing with if I got into the side, I told myself. No, *when* I got into the side. I wasn't going to throw this chance away. But I had to meet the coach first. That was why I was here.

Jules had told me that the coach was called Joe. I watched him running up and down the pitch, yelling at the players. Some of them were practising ball control, and some of them were banging the ball into the net, one after the other. I wondered how Joe felt, being the only guy out there. He didn't seem to mind, though. He seemed pretty much at home . . . And kind of good-looking – if you're interested in that sort of thing.

I took a deep breath, and ran out on to the pitch. Jules had stopped to chat to Joe as I rushed over to them. The first thing I noticed was that Joe didn't look too pleased to see me. But that couldn't stop me grinning from ear to ear. I was excited just to *be* there.

'Where do you usually play?' Joe said. No hello, nothing. It would have sounded really off, if he hadn't had such a soft Irish accent.

I beamed at him. 'In the park.'

He looked at Jules and frowned. 'I meant, what position?'

'Oh, sorry.' I felt a bit of a fool. 'I usually play all over, but up front on the right is best.'

Joe looked me up and down. 'Get your boots on, then,' he said.

My face fell. 'I haven't got any.'

For a minute, I thought he was going to chuck me out before I'd even got started. I stared at him anxiously, trying to make him realise how desperate I was to play. Jules was looking a bit uncomfortable. I guessed that she'd had to persuade Joe to give me a go.

'All right,' he said at last. 'Join in and start warming up.'

I smiled with relief, and unzipped my tracksuit

top. I had my Beckham shirt on underneath. Maybe soon I'd be wearing the Harriers strip like the other girls. But first I had to show what I could do . . .

I felt nervous as I took my place on the pitch with the other players. I never felt nervous when I was playing against Taz and that lot, but this was different. I had to do well to earn a place in the side.

But once the ball was at my feet, I lost all my nerves. It was just like being back in the park. Adrenaline pumped through me as I dribbled down the pitch, managing to avoid two defenders. I did my famous double-step over the ball to get round a third and ran forward. I had the goal in my sights.

'Pass to Jules!' I heard Joe yelling from the touchline.

I slid the ball across the box, straight into Jules' path, and she sidefooted it into the net.

'Brilliant!' Joe called, and I glowed with pride. I wanted this so much it *hurt*.

When the game was over, I was so nervous, I felt sick. I wanted to know if I'd made it into the side. I *thought* I'd done well – I hadn't scored myself, but I'd set up goals for Jules and another girl whose name I didn't know. As we trooped off the pitch, I felt my heart lurch as Joe came over to me and took me to one side.

'How'd it feel out there?' he asked.

'Excellent,' I gasped. I was red in the face and out of breath, but I felt fantastic. 'Really great.'

Joe looked at me curiously. 'I've never seen an Indian girl into football.'

I smiled shyly at him. 'I would have come sooner, but I didn't even know they had a girls' team here.'

'It's all her fault,' Joe said. He nodded at Jules who'd run over to join us. 'When I was playing for the men's club, she used to hang around whining that there was no team for her.'

'I wasn't *whining*,' Jules argued. 'But there was nothing for us girls. Just junior league boys' stuff. But when he busted his knee and couldn't play any more, he set up a girls' side –' she grinned at Joe, and I realised, with a bit of a shock, that she had the hots for him '– and he's been on my case ever since.'

'I really want to coach the men's side, but the club made me start at the bottom,' Joe said. It was the first time I'd seen him really smile. 'And you can't get much lower than her.'

'Oh, you're so full of it!' Jules laughed. I was beginning to feel a bit left out. She and Joe obviously got on pretty well. 'We win just as many trophies as the men's side. So . . .' She flung an arm round my shoulders. 'Does she pass?'

I looked eagerly at Joe.

'Your folks up for it?' he asked.

I looked as innocent as I could. 'Oh, yeah, they're cool.' No way was I admitting the truth.

'Right, you'd better come back then.' Joe leaned over and punched Jules playfully on the shoulder. 'And I suppose I'd better go and open the bar. Do some real work.'

He went off towards the clubhouse. I glanced at Jules. She could hardly take her eyes off him. Actually, I didn't really blame her. He *was* a great coach.

Jules turned to me. 'He likes you.'

For no reason at all, I blushed. 'You think so?'

'He asked you back, didn't he?' Jules grinned. 'How long have you been playing?'

I shrugged. 'Oh, for ages, but nothing as serious as this. Just in the park.'

'Serious, this?' Jules laughed. 'It'll do for now, but I want to play professionally.'

My mouth fell open in amazement. 'Wow! You can *do* that?' I gasped. 'As a job, you mean?'

'Sure.' Jules nodded. 'Not really here, but you can in America. They've got a pro-league there with new stadiums and everything.'

'Really?' I couldn't believe what I was hearing. Women could play football professionally? Suddenly, becoming a boring old solicitor seemed even less interesting than it had before. Jules was lucky, I thought enviously. Her mum and dad must really support her to let her go all the way to America to play. I felt a stab of anxiety. And here I was not even knowing how to tell mine about Hounslow Harriers . . .

THREE

'Here.' Joe handed me a pair of boots. 'They're a bit tatty, but they'll do the job.'

I couldn't stop myself grinning. I didn't care *how* tatty they were. They were my first real pair of football boots. And not my last, I hoped.

'Thanks,' I said, taking them and weighing them up in my hands.

'And here's the kit,' Joe went on, shoving a Harriers shirt and a pair of shorts into my arms. 'Don't be afraid to get it dirty.'

My smile disappeared fast. I held up the shorts and looked at them in dismay. I don't do shorts. Ever.

'Can't I wear my tracksuit bottoms?' I blurted out.

Joe was already walking away towards the pitch. 'No. Go and get changed.'

My heart sank. I stared at the shorts. They looked tiny – my scar would be totally visible. I couldn't believe he was making me do this. I sighed and headed towards the changing-rooms.

I nearly died when I walked inside. The changing-room was packed – and most of the girls had half their clothes off. One was actually walking round in her bra and knickers, without a care in the world. I gulped, clutching my kit. I wasn't used to undressing in public. It just wasn't something we did in my family. And my scar didn't help. But I was just going to have to get on with it. This was a whole new world I was jumping into.

'Hey, Jess.' Jules called to me from across the room. 'Get changed over here with me.'

I hurried over gratefully. She looked really pleased to see me, which was reassuring. 'You've met our captain, Mel, haven't you?' she went on.

A pretty black girl was getting changed next to Jules. 'Yeah,' I smiled. 'Hi.'

'So you're up for a proper match then, Jess,' Mel said with a friendly grin. 'Chiswick next. They've got the best defensive record in the division, so they're due for a good stuffing.' She pulled her T-shirt over her head. 'We need some pace up front.' I nodded, trying to look anywhere other than at her chest. 'And Jules could do with some decent service. So, welcome to the Harriers, Jess!'

'Thanks,' I mumbled.

It was about time I started getting changed too, so I slipped my Harriers shirt over my head and began trying to get my sweatshirt off underneath. I was tying myself up in knots, so I was glad when the other girls started filing outside. Within a few minutes I was the only one left in the dressing-room.

I whipped off my tracksuit bottoms, and pulled on the shorts. I felt sick. I hardly ever looked at my scar, and I'd forgotten just how big and ugly it was. It ran all the way down my right thigh to my knee. The shorts hardly covered it at all.

I crept out of the changing-rooms, trying vainly to pull the right leg of my shorts down to hide the scar. Out on the pitch, Joe had already started the team jogging on the ball. I was dying to join in, but I just couldn't bring myself to. Maybe if I talked to him again, he'd let me wear my tracksuit bottoms instead.

I slipped into the stand and sat down. After a moment or two Joe spotted me and walked over, frowning.

'Jess, what's going on?'

I didn't answer, so he vaulted over the barrier and came to sit beside me. I watched his face to see his expression when he noticed my scar. He looked totally taken aback. But he didn't seem disgusted or anything.

'It looks awful,' I muttered. 'That's why I can't wear shorts.'

'Jesus, that's a stunner all right,' Joe agreed. 'I thought I had a bad one on my knee, but yours is gorgeous! Look,' he went on gently, 'don't worry about it. No-one's going to care once you're out there.' He glanced down at my leg again. 'What happened?'

'You don't want to know,' I said gloomily.

Joe pulled up the leg of his tracksuit and showed me a scar on his right knee. 'Two operations later, and it's still useless,' he said. 'Does yours affect your game?'

I shook my head. 'Nah, it just looks awful.' I glanced across at him. 'I was eight. My mum was working overtime at Heathrow so I thought I'd help and make my own dinner. Beans on toast. But when I jumped up to get the toast from the grill, my trousers caught fire.' I shivered as I remembered the shock and the pain. 'My sister put me in the bath, poured cold water over me and pulled my trousers off.' I screwed my face up. 'But half my skin came off too.'

'I'm sorry,' Joe said quietly.

'I know,' I sighed. 'Put me off beans on toast for life.'

He burst out laughing and stood up. 'C'mon. Mine stopped me from playing outright. Yours doesn't.'

I felt a bit ashamed of myself, then. Joe was right. At least I could still play.

'I'm sorry about your knee,' I said hesitantly.

'Yeah, yeah, I'm a right sob story, aren't I?' Joe shrugged, as we walked out on to the pitch. I noticed Jules looking at us a bit strangely. She was probably wondering what we were talking about. 'Now, come on, let's see some sweat on you.'

I couldn't get over how understanding Joe was. He seemed to know exactly how I was feeling inside. He really was a brilliant coach. I bet he'd been an ace player, too. It was a shame about his knee injury.

Seconds later I'd forgotten all about my stupid scar. I joined the others jogging on the ball, then we set the hurdles up and Joe got us to jump over them with our feet together. I was worried that I might not be as fit as the rest of them, but all that running rings round Taz and the others in the park seemed to have paid off. I was a bit out of breath, but not much.

After some more fitness training, we moved on to practising ball skills. We had to stand in a long line with a ball each and dribble from one side of the pitch to the other, without knocking into anyone.

Then Joe set up some barriers and got Jules and me to practise bending the ball round them, just like Beckham. He was better than both of us, but I wasn't too bad. I'd watched enough videos of Beckham, winding and re-winding to study his technique.

We finished off the training session with a quick game, and this time I scored myself as well as setting two up for Jules. As I ran home afterwards, I was buzzing. I didn't feel tired at all. I could've run to Old Trafford and back! *This* was what I'd always wanted to do. And now that I'd got used to the kit, I couldn't bear to take it off. I didn't care if the whole of London saw my scar. I was on a total high.

The boys were playing in the park as usual. I dashed over to them, grinning all over my face. 'Hey, Tony!'

Tony stared at me admiringly. 'Wow, Jess! You look like a pro in that kit.'

'It's brilliant, Tony,' I gabbled happily. 'They're a top team, and the coach is ace.'

'Excellent!'

The other boys had stopped playing and were staring at me.

'What's that down your leg?' Taz said, pointing at my scar.

'Haven't you seen a burn before?' I retorted.

All the boys made loud noises like they were about to be sick.

'That's disgusting, man!' Taz pulled a face.

'Oi!' Tony yelled, squaring up to him. 'Back off, you prat.'

'Ooh, lover boy!' they all sniggered, and fell about laughing.

'It's fine.' I was eyeing the ball at Taz's feet. 'At least I can still beat you with my eyes closed!' I darted forward and nicked the ball. Taz raced after me, but I nutmegged him totally – I backheeled the ball between his legs, then turned and picked it up behind him. Taz gave a shout of frustration. He doubled back and came at me again. This time I stopped the ball dead before he got to me and whipped it round out of his reach.

'Oh, skill!' I shouted, as I ran off down the pitch. I was really enjoying myself. 'Look at the skill!'

I came to a full stop as Taz grabbed me round the waist from behind, and lifted me up into the air.

'Put me down!' I yelled.

The boys were all roaring with laughter as Taz swung me over his shoulder like a fireman. I was laughing too – until I saw the look on Tony's face.

He was staring past me and Taz, but I couldn't see what he was looking at. The other boys stopped laughing too. Then Taz glanced round, and dropped me on the grass like a hot potato.

My mum was standing there with a bag of groceries in her hand, looking like she was about to skin me alive.

'Chi! Chi!' Mum was wringing her hands, standing in front of the picture of Guru Nanak. 'He was touching you all over, putting his hands on your bare legs.' She glared at me. I was sitting on the sofa, still wearing my Harriers kit. 'You're not a young girl any more, Jesminder. And you showing the world your scar . . . *Hai Bhagvan* . . .'

'Jessie, now that your sister's engaged, it's different,' said Dad. He was at the bar in the corner, getting himself a whisky. I didn't drink, but right now I could have done with one myself. 'You know how our people talk.'

'*She's* the one getting married, not me!' I said resentfully.

'*I* was married at your age,' Mum snapped. 'You don't even want to learn how to cook *daal*!'

I didn't see what that had to do with it. 'Anyway,

I'm not playing with boys any more.' Maybe *that* would shut them up.

'Good.' Mum headed off towards the kitchen. '*Gaal kuthum*, end of matter.'

'I'm joining a girls' team,' I went on. 'They want me to play in proper matches.'

Mum and Dad stared at each other.

'The coach said I could go far,' I added, looking hopefully at Dad. He was always more of a soft touch than Mum.

'Go far?' Mum snorted. 'To where? Jessie, we let you play all you wanted when you were young. You've played enough.'

'But that's not fair,' I cut in. 'He selected me.'

'He?' Mum pounced like a cat on a mouse, and turned to Dad. 'She said it was girls!'

'The coach is called Joe,' I explained patiently.

'See how she lies?' Mum shook her head at Dad. 'What family will want a daughter-in-law who can run around kicking a football all day, but can't make round *chapattis*?' She looked sternly at me. 'Now your exams are over, I want you to learn full Punjabi dinner. Meat *and* vegetarian!'

'But, Dad—' I began.

Dad started to say something, but Mum jumped

in again. 'Look, this is how you spoil her,' she said loudly. 'This is how it started with your niece. The way that girl would answer back! Then she runs off to become a model wearing small-small skirts.'

'Mum!' I tried to get a word in edgeways. 'She's a fashion designer!'

'She's *divorced*, that's what she is,' Mum pointed out triumphantly. 'Cast off after three years married to a *gora* with blue hair! Her poor mother, she hasn't been able to set foot in the temple since. I don't want this shame in my family.' She held up her hand. 'That's it. No more football!'

She stormed off to the kitchen. I slumped on the sofa. I couldn't believe it. I'd finally found something I really wanted to do and now I wasn't going to be allowed to do it.

'Jessie, your mother's right,' Dad said, looking at me awkwardly. 'It doesn't look nice. You must behave like a proper young woman now.'

There was no point in arguing. I swallowed hard, trying not to cry. It looked like my footballing days were well and truly over.

* * *

'It's out of order, Tony!' I bunched my wet hanky into a ball, and scrubbed at my eyes. 'Anything I want is just not Indian enough for them. I mean, I never bunked off school like Pinky and Bubbly, I don't wear make-up or tarty clothes like them. But they just don't *see* all those things.'

'Parents *never* see the good things,' Tony said understandingly. We were walking through the park together. After what had happened, I'd just had to get out of the house.

'*Anyone* can cook *aloo gobi*,' I muttered. 'But who can bend a ball like Beckham?'

Tony looked thoughtfully at me. He was dribbling a football along as we walked. 'Why don't you just play, and not tell them?' he suggested. 'I mean, Pinky's been sneaking off for years to see Teets, and now they're getting married, no-one cares. What your parents don't know won't hurt 'em.'

'Why should I have to lie?' I sighed. 'It's not like I'm sleeping around or anything.'

'Jess!'

Jules was running to catch us up. Quickly I wiped my eyes again. 'Hi, Jules,' I said, as cheerfully as I could. 'This is Tony. Tony, this is Jules from the team.'

'Hi, all right?' Tony grinned at her. 'Jess's made up with your team.'

'We've got high hopes for her,' Jules smiled back. 'Especially me.'

I looked down at the ground. 'My mum doesn't want me to play any more,' I blurted out.

'What?! But that's crap!' Jules sounded horrified. 'Listen, my mum's never wanted *me* to play since I started. You just can't take no for an answer.'

I glanced at her. 'Really?'

Jules nodded. 'Yeah, she's convinced I'm too much of a tomboy. She's always trying to make me wear girly clothes, and go out with this bloke we know called Kevin. And do you know what she said to me the other day –' Jules put on a posh voice '– "Honey, I'm telling you there's a *reason* why Sporty Spice is the only one of them without a fella!" Honestly, can you believe that?'

'But my sister's getting married soon, and my parents are totally stressed out,' I explained. 'I won't be able to get out of the house for training and matches anyway.'

'Come on, Jess, you can't leave me alone out there,' Jules urged. 'Joe's told me he's got an American scout coming over.'

I remembered what Jules said about the American Pro-League, and felt a stab of envy. That was never going to happen for *me*.

'Anyway, don't worry about your mum,' Jules went on confidently. 'Just tell her you've got a summer job. Say you're working at HMV with me.'

That was a great idea. I glanced at Tony, who nodded. It might just work.

'So, now we've got *that* sorted –' Jules grinned widely at us and nicked the ball from Tony '– are you going to show me what your fella can do or what?'

'Oh, he's not my fella,' I said, at exactly the same time as Tony said, 'I'm not her boyfriend.'

We looked at each other, embarrassed, and then Tony scooted off after Jules.

'Come on, Jess,' Jules yelled over her shoulder. 'Are you playing or what?'

I ran after them. I felt better, but not much. I was going to carry on playing, but I was going to have to lie to do it. I didn't know if I could pull it off.

FOUR

'Jessie! Breakfast!'

'Mum, I'm in a hurry,' I yelled from my bedroom.

'You can't go to work on an empty stomach.' Mum bustled out of the kitchen carrying a plate of bread and butter, as I ran down the stairs. Behind her Pinky was rushing about in her uniform, moaning that she couldn't find her keys. She's a rep on the Avis car rental desk at Heathrow, and she's always late.

'No, I've got to go, Mum,' I said firmly, waving the food away. 'Bye.' I wanted to be well away from the house before Pinky left for work.

I slammed the front door behind me, and hurried over to the flower border at the side of the path. I pulled out my sports bag, which I'd hidden there the night before, then legged it.

I'd been doing this for about a week now. Mum, Dad and Pinky thought I was working at HMV. Instead, I was at the Harriers ground. I felt really bad about lying – as well as scared stiff that someone would see me somewhere they shouldn't. I kept telling myself it wasn't like I was doing anything wrong. I mean, I wasn't going around doing drugs or getting pregnant or shoplifting or anything. I was just playing football, trying to get better at something I was already good at.

And I *was* getting better. Joe was such a brilliant coach, it was impossible not to learn from him. He spent a lot of time with me and Jules, working on our partnership and teaching us one-two moves that we could use on the pitch. He worked us pretty hard, but the three of us had a good laugh too. The more we trained together, the more I liked him.

Jules was always flirting with him, and staring at him when we were training. Joe would've been blind not to notice, but he never gave any sign that he had. I wondered if he fancied her too. I couldn't tell. Still, it wasn't really any of my business . . .

The day our first match of the summer tournament against Chiswick came round, I felt nervous, but I couldn't wait to get out on to the pitch. This wasn't like playing in the park, or the games in our training sessions. This was the real thing.

'All right, Jess?' Joe asked me quietly as we filed out of the changing-rooms.

I blushed, and Jules, who was just ahead of me,

turned round curiously to look at us. Don't ask me why I went red, I don't know – I just did. 'Yeah, no problem,' I muttered.

'OK, go out there and do your stuff,' Joe said, and turned away.

And, suddenly, when I was out on the pitch, everything seemed to come together. Joining the Harriers had been the best thing in my whole life so far, and I'd loved the training sessions, pushing myself harder and getting better and better. But out on the pitch, playing a real game, was what it was all about. Adrenaline raced through me as the ball was placed in the centre circle, ready for the kick-off. I was up for this, and I was going to do my best.

Mel was right. Chiswick had a great defence, and it took us a while to break them down. About halfway through the second half, Jules slotted the ball through to me, opening up a gap between two defenders. I ran through and banged the ball into the net. One-nil.

'Yes!' I yelled. My first goal in a proper, real-life match! I was so excited, I cartwheeled across the pitch and finished off with a back-flip. As the other girls rushed to congratulate me, I looked over at Joe. He was grinning at me, and I glowed with pride.

By the time we'd won the match two-nil, with another goal from Mel, I knew that there was no going back. I couldn't give this up. Even if I *did* have to lie to keep on playing.

After that, I began to relax a bit, and the days settled into a routine. Most mornings I'd get up, collect my sports bag from behind the bush, and dash off to training. Afterwards I'd give my dirty kit to Jules, and she'd take it home to wash. The team were still playing in the first few rounds of the tournament, and we had several more matches. We won them all, and I either scored myself, or managed to set up goals for Jules or one of the others. When we had evening games, it was more difficult for me to get away, though – I had to tell Mum I was doing overtime at work. Luckily no-one at home seemed to notice that I was just as skint now as I when I started my 'summer job'!

I was getting on better with Mum too, because I'd agreed to learn how to cook. She wasn't too pleased, though, when she saw me practising my **ball** skills with a potato when we were cooking *aloo gobi*. I just couldn't help it. Football was consuming my life.

But everything seemed to be going brilliantly. My

parents were happy, the team was happy – I was happy. It was perfect.

You know what?

It couldn't last.

A few weeks later, I was in the changing-rooms, getting dressed after a training session. I'd kind of got used to getting changed in front of the others now, and I didn't feel uncomfortable sitting there in my sports bra and shorts next to Jules, while I took off my boots.

'Is that right then, Jess?' Charlie, the goalie, asked me as she towelled her hair dry. 'Your parents have no idea you've been playing all this time?'

I shrugged. 'Nah, they haven't.' Now that I felt more comfortable around the other girls, I'd let them in on my little secret.

'Where do they think you are, then?' Mel asked.

'At work.' I pulled off one of my boots. 'They think I've got a summer job at HMV.'

'Blimey.' Mel looked a bit startled. 'That's not on.'

'Indian girls aren't supposed to play football,' I explained helpfully.

'That's a bit backward, innit?' Mel remarked, picking up her towel.

'Yeah, but it ain't just an Indian thing, is it?' Jules cut in. 'I mean, how many people come out to support us?'

Mel ignored her and grinned at me. 'So, are you, like, *promised* to someone, then?'

'Nah,' I said, looking alarmed. All the other girls in the changing-room were listening now too. 'No way. My sister's getting married soon, but that's a love match.'

'What's that mean?'

'It's not arranged,' I replied.

'So, if you can choose,' Charlie said, looking interested, 'can you marry a white boy?'

I shook my head. 'White, no. Black, definitely not. Muslim—' I drew my finger across my throat.

Mel and the others looked shocked.

'So you'll probably marry an Indian boy, then?' Jules asked, packing our kit away in her sports bag.

'Probably.'

Mel was shaking her head. 'I don't know how you put up with it.'

I shrugged. 'It's just my culture, that's all,' I said defensively. 'Anyway, it's better than sleeping around with boys you're not going to end up marrying. What's the point in that?'

They all burst out laughing.

'That's the best bit!' giggled Sally, one of our defenders.

'Yeah, you should know,' Charlie retorted.

They all laughed even harder. I turned pink, and bent over to do up my trainers.

'When are you going to get some decent boots, Jess?' Jules asked, as we went outside. 'You want some Adidas ones like mine. They're especially made for women.'

'They look a bit pricey,' I said doubtfully, but I was thinking hard. If I was going to take my game seriously, I really should get some new boots. At the moment, I was still using the tatty ones Joe had given me. There must be a way I could get the money for some new ones . . .

I headed for home, dumped my bag in the flower border as usual and went inside. Mum was sitting on the sofa. She was doing some sewing and watching a Hindi film with Amitabh Bachchan, her favourite actor. I was knackered, and dying for something to eat.

'Mum,' I said in my sweetest voice, 'I'm *really* starving. I had to work all through my lunch hour today.'

Mum had been fussing around me ever since I started my 'summer job' so I was hoping she'd get up and make a meal. Instead, she just stared at me.

'Where's Pinky?' she asked, looking over my shoulder at the front door. 'She went to HMV to pick you up, so you wouldn't be late for Poli. She's coming to measure you for the wedding suits.'

My stomach flipped over, and my heart began to pound. It was so loud, I was surprised Mum couldn't hear it. I was desperately trying to think of an explanation which would cover me, when the front door opened.

Total panic. I looked round as Pinky came in, looking pissed off. She gave me a filthy look, and I gulped.

Was she going to give me away?

FIVE

I stared pleadingly at Pinky, as she shut the front door. If she told Mum I hadn't been working at HMV at all, I was going to be in *big* trouble. No, wipe that – HUGE trouble. They'd probably never let me set foot outside the house again.

'Pinky, why didn't you pick your sister up from work?' Mum asked, rolling up her sewing.

'I went, but the manager said I'd just missed her,' Pinky replied, staring hard at me.

I'd been holding my breath, and now I let it out with a sigh of relief. I was safe – for the moment.

'Poli's on her way.' Mum got up from the sofa. 'I'll make you girls some tea.'

Pinky waited till Mum had gone into the kitchen, then she grabbed my arm, dragged me off the sofa, and hustled me into the corner of the room, as far away from Mum as she could get.

'All right,' she whispered eagerly. 'Who is he, then?'

I looked blank. I'd been expecting her to have a go at me. 'Who?'

'You must think I'm stupid or something,' Pinky snapped. 'I know what you're up to, lying about a summer job!'

'You can't say anything to Mum and Dad,' I gabbled, panicking all over again. 'Remember, I kept Teets a secret for you.'

Pinky suddenly looked worried. 'He's not a Muslim, is he?'

I shook my head. 'Ssh! Nothing like that. I've been playing football with a women's team.'

Pinky's eyes widened, and she looked at me as if I was mad. 'It's worse than I thought,' she muttered.

'It's a proper tournament,' I explained. 'They're real matches.'

Pinky grabbed my arm again. 'What's *wrong* with you, Jess?' she hissed, looking completely puzzled. 'If you're gonna go to all this bother lying, at least do it for something good! Don't you want a boyfriend like everyone else?'

I sighed, rolling my eyes. Why was it so impossible for her to understand?

'You know, you're quite pretty,' Pinky went on, studying my face intently. 'If you just did something with your hair and put a bit of make-up on, you'd look all right.'

'Leave her alone, Pinky.' We both jumped as Mum came in with two mugs of tea. 'I never put make-up on till after I was married. Jessie's a good girl now.' She beamed at me. 'She helped me to wash all the net curtains, and she made lovely *aloo gobi* last week.'

I smiled back at Mum, feeling a bit guilty. Luckily, Poli arrived just then, which got Pinky off my case. She would never understand why I was going behind Mum and Dad's back to play football, and there wasn't any point in me trying to explain it to her. Just as long as she kept my secret. And it looked as if she was going to, thank God.

Poli was the seamstress who made most of our Indian clothes. She bustled round, unpacking her tape measure and chatting to Mum in Punjabi. Pinky stood up to be measured first, while I sat thinking about how I could get my hands on some new football boots. I had a bit of money, but not enough for the Adidas ones.

'Waist, 25 inches,' Poli muttered, wrapping the tape measure round Pinky. 'Under bust, 28 inches. Bust—'

Pinky grabbed hold of the tape measure and pulled it tighter. Mum frowned at her.

'No, that's too tight and too rude,' she complained.

'Nah, Mum,' Pinky argued. 'I want my sari blouse more fitted. That's the style, innit?'

'OK.' Poli pulled the tape measure tighter. 'Bust, 34 and a half.'

'Tighter,' Pinky whispered.

'And how are you going to breathe?' Mum snapped.

I was my turn. I dragged myself up reluctantly from the sofa. 'Mum, I can wear the same suit all day,' I moaned. 'Why do I have to wear a sari for the reception? It'll just fall down.'

'Your first sari is for when you become a woman,' Mum retorted. 'Poli, she needs a sari blouse and petticoat.'

Poli started measuring me. 'Bust, 31 inches—'

'No, that's too tight,' I said quickly. 'I want it looser.'

Mum snorted. 'Dressed in a sack, who's going to notice you?'

'Don't worry,' Poli said. 'In one of our designs, even these mosquito bites will look like juicy-juicy mangoes!'

The three of them burst out laughing, while I pulled a face. But an idea had suddenly popped into my head . . .

'Mum,' I began innocently, 'I'll need to buy different shoes, then. One pair to go with the sari and the other to go with my suit.'

'What?' Pinky said, looking stunned.

Mum turned to her. 'You see, she's coming into line,' she murmured approvingly.

'I can pay for one pair myself out of my wages,' I went on hopefully, 'but could you give me some money for the other pair?'

Mum beamed and nodded. 'You need one black pair and one white to go with everything.'

She, Pinky and Poli looked delightedly at me. What they *didn't* know was that I was planning to spend almost all the money on football boots – and they *definitely* wouldn't go with my new suit or my sari . . .

'Those are the ones, Jess!' Jules said gleefully, looking down at the pair of black, white and red Adidas Predators I was holding.

I nodded, excitement welling up inside me. We were in *Soccer Scene* in Carnaby Street. We'd gone to Hounslow Central and caught the tube into the West End after training, so that I could buy myself some boots. Now, as I tried them on, I was beginning to feel like a real player at last.

'OK, I'll take them,' I said at last. I handed over the money, then took the precious bag. I couldn't stop peeking inside at them. My very own pair of flash football boots!

'Where shall we go now?' I asked, as we came out of the shop.

'Haven't you got to buy some shoes for the wedding?' Jules reminded me.

I pulled a face. 'Yeah, but I've only got fifteen quid left.' The boots had been more expensive than I'd thought.

'What about that place over there?' Jules pointed at a nearby shop called *Stylish Shoes*. 'That looks cheap and nasty.'

'Thanks a lot!' I laughed.

It *was* cheap. I got a pair of black loafers for £13.99. That should shut Mum up, I thought with satisfaction as we left the shop. Now I just had to make sure I kept my new boots out of her way.

'I don't really want to go home yet,' Jules said, as we headed back through the side streets. She stopped outside a pub called *The Three Greyhounds*. 'Let's have a drink.'

'I can't go in there,' I said nervously. I'd never been

in a pub in my life. 'Someone I know might see me.'

'Aw, come on, Jess.' Jules took my arm and dragged me inside. She sat me down at a table and went to the bar while I looked around the smoke-filled pub nervously. Once I was sure there were no Indian guys around, I relaxed a bit.

Jules came back with a lager for herself and a Coke for me. I couldn't help envying her. She seemed so sure of herself. She knew exactly what she wanted to do and where she was going. And here was me who'd never been in a pub before, who'd never even drunk alcohol either.

'When's this American scout coming, then?' I asked her, remembering what she'd said when we were in the park.

Jules shrugged. 'Dunno.' She lifted her glass and took a drink. 'But I hope it's soon. You know what really pisses me off, Jess? There's no money in the women's game over here. We're *years* behind America.'

'But America never get anywhere in the World Cup,' I pointed out.

'That's the blokes,' Jules replied. 'The girls are mad for it. The US's women's team, right, they went on *strike* to demand that they got paid the same as the men.' She grinned at me. 'And they won! One of our England team even drives a taxi to pay her way. Can you see Beckham having to do that?'

I shook my head. 'I still can't believe that women get paid for playing football.'

'Mia Hamm, one of the American players, makes *millions* in sponsorship,' Jules said, a serious look on her face. 'And I want to be up there with her. I've got a place at Loughborough doing sports education, but if Joe does get that American scout over . . .' She shrugged. 'Who knows?'

'You're so lucky,' I said enviously. 'I can't even leave home to go to college. I have to go to Kingston Uni if I get my grades.'

Jules looked me straight in the eye. 'And is that what you really *want* to do?' she asked.

I couldn't say anything. I knew what I *wanted* to do, and it was exactly the same as Jules. Go to America and become a professional player and earn loads of money doing the one thing I loved. The problem was, I knew that I'd never be allowed to do it.

'Mum, she's back!'

Shut up, Pinky, I cursed silently as I hurried into

the house. Mum and Dad were sitting on the sofa, and Pinky was in the kitchen, so she'd spotted me fumbling with my key outside the front door. I'd been hoping to slide in quietly without any fuss, shoot upstairs and shove my boots under the bed where nobody would see them.

'Jesminder!' Mum turned round and stared at me. 'You've been gone all day for two pairs of shoes? Come here.'

'It's not that late, Mum,' I said, edging towards the stairs. 'I was looking at other things too, like –' I had to think for a minute '– handbags.'

Pinky came out of the kitchen, and raised her eyebrows. 'Let me see 'em,' she demanded.

'Not yet,' I gabbled. 'I'll try them on with my suit.'

I headed for the stairs. I made it about halfway up, but Pinky ran after me and grabbed the carrier bag. I raced down the stairs after her, but she jumped on to the sofa between Mum and Dad, and handed the carrier bag to Mum. My heart sank. I leaned over the sofa, trying to get the bag back, but suddenly Mum grabbed my jacket and pulled me closer. Then she started sniffing me like a mad thing.

'Have you been *smoking*?' she asked furiously.

'No!' I gasped. I groaned inwardly, remembering

how smoky the pub had been. I must stink of cigarettes, and Mum's got a nose like a bloodhound.

'Chi chi!' Mum moaned, sniffing me again. 'Cigarettes *and* drink!'

'Look, I had to go to the loo, so I went into a pub with my friend,' I gabbled. 'I had a Coke – look, you can smell my breath.'

Dad jumped up from the sofa and came round to sniff at me. 'She could be right,' he admitted.

Mum looked slightly less stressed. That didn't last long though. She opened the first shoe box and took out the black loafers. She stared at them in disgust, and Pinky pulled a face.

'These don't even have any heel,' Mum pointed out crossly. 'How will your sari fall nicely in these?'

'I'll take them back,' I mumbled, desperate to stop them opening the second shoe box. 'Give me the bag.'

But it was too late. Mum already had the other box opened, and was holding an Adidas Predator in her hand. '*Football* shoes,' she wailed, and buried her face against the boot as if she was about to burst into tears.

'You can't take them back, Jess,' Jules said firmly. The

whole team was on the grass doing sit-ups. We were in two long lines facing each other, and Jules was opposite me.

'I've got to,' I muttered. The hassle I'd got was unbelievable. I'd been warned again that football was out. Luckily, my parents hadn't realised that I'd been playing all this time for the Harriers without them knowing, and Pinky had kept her mouth shut too. 'Mum told me I had to take them back and get some proper shoes for the wedding.'

'Don't worry about it,' Jules said between gasps. 'Come to my house after this, and I'll sort you out.'

'Come on, girls,' Joe yelled. He was standing at the top of the two lines, keeping a sharp eye on us. 'Wake up!'

'God, my mum had a fit when she saw the boots,' I grumbled. 'And I smelt like a bleeding ashtray too. They made me wash up all the big saucepans after dinner. Yuk.'

'Yak, yak, yak, Jess!'

I looked up to find Joe staring hard at me.

'Everything all right?' he asked in a softer voice.

'Yes, coach,' I said.

'Training getting in the way of your cosy little conversation?' he enquired.

'No, coach,' I said nervously.

'Good!' he shouted, making me jump. 'So you won't mind five more laps round the pitch, then. Elbows to knees as you go.'

I got to my feet, wishing he hadn't said that. My right ankle was hurting me at the moment, and it had got worse during training. But I wasn't going to argue.

That didn't stop Jules, though. 'Joe, that's totally out of order!' she exclaimed.

'I don't remember telling the rest of you to stop,' I heard Joe shout as I ran off around the pitch, lifting my knees up high. 'C'mon, move it! You're doing really well. Just keep it up for the next fifteen minutes.'

I carried on running round the pitch. My ankle twinged every so often and I winced. It felt as though I'd sprained it slightly. But I was determined to keep going.

The training session finished just as I was completing my fourth lap, and I watched the other girls going back to the changing-room. My ankle was really beginning to hurt now and I was limping.

'All right, Jess.' Joe came running over to me, looking concerned. 'You can stop now.'

'No, I'm OK,' I panted. 'I've just got one more lap.'

'I said, Stop,' Joe said sternly. 'You're doing yourself an injury.' He took my arm. 'Come on, let's have a look at you.'

'It's nothing . . .'

'Sit down.' Joe pointed at the grass. 'And let me decide if it's nothing or not.'

I eased myself down on to the grass, biting my lip. Joe knelt down and undid my boot, then he slipped my sock off gently. I felt hot all over. I knew I was red in the face, and it wasn't just because I'd been running either.

'Why didn't you tell me you'd twisted it?' Joe asked. He put his hand on the sole of my foot and rotated it gently.

'I didn't want you to think I wasn't as strong as the others,' I muttered. The feel of his warm hand on my bare skin was doing weird things to my insides.

Joe shook his head. 'That's stupid, Jess. Look, my dad was my coach and the scouts kept telling him I was too slight to play, but he kept pushing me. That's how I injured my knee.'

'You mean, your dad made you?' I asked softly.

'I wanted to show him I wasn't soft,' Joe replied. 'So I tried to play injured.' His face shadowed. 'He always was a bastard, anyway.'

'You shouldn't say that about your dad,' I murmured.

Joe glanced up at me, and my heart started to thunder in my ears. 'You don't know my dad.'

He helped me up, then put one arm round my shoulder and the other round my waist. I froze, and just about managed to stop myself gasping aloud. It was the closest I'd ever been to a boy before. And I was enjoying it. If Taz or Sonny or any of the others, even Tony, had tried it, I would probably have punched them on the nose. But this was different. The way I felt about Joe was different.

I was falling for him.

And I couldn't do a damn thing about it.

SIX

I stared intently at the photo of Joe and Jules on the dressing-table. Jules had left me in her bedroom, while she went to nick a pair of her mum's shoes for me to borrow. I'd been studying the posters of women footballers on the walls, when I'd spotted the photo. Jules and Joe had their arms wrapped round each other, and they looked really happy, as if they were celebrating. I felt a bit jealous, although I tried not to be. Nothing was going to happen between me and Joe anyway. He was white, for a start. It was OK for me to hang around with Jules, because we were just friends. But I could just imagine my parents' faces if I brought Joe home to tea and said he was my boyfriend.

The way I felt about Joe had kind of shocked me. I'd never thought about a boy that way before, and it had sort of crept up on me without me noticing. My head was spinning as I tried to analyse exactly *why* I liked him. OK, he was good-looking, but it wasn't just that. It was the way he understood exactly why I loved playing football, and how important it was to me. We were on the same wavelength.

I was still staring dreamily at the photo when a pair of black, high-heeled shoes with diamante bows were suddenly thrust under my nose.

'Just give 'em back after the wedding,' Jules said with a grin. 'My mum loves them. She stuck the bows on herself, would you believe.'

The shoes were a bit fussy for me, but Mum would like them, so at least they would shut her up. 'Are you sure your mum won't miss them?' I asked.

Jules shrugged. 'Nah, she's got a million pairs.' She hesitated for a moment, then went on. 'Listen, I hope Joe isn't too hard on you. Some of the girls think he's strict.'

'Oh no,' I said, knowing that I was blushing. 'He was really nice.' That sounded like I fancied him, so I quickly added, 'Really professional.'

I glanced at the photo again, wanting to ask Jules if she really did have the hots for him. But I was too shy.

Jules followed my gaze, and her face lit up. 'Oh, I love that picture,' she said. 'It was taken just after we beat Millwall last year.' Smiling to herself, she went over to the TV and switched it on. 'Come on, you've got to see this. It's wicked!'

A logo appeared on the TV screen – *Women's United Soccer Association*. I gasped as the picture switched to a large American stadium full of fans, watching a match between two women's teams.

'Wow! That's amazing!'

'Yeah, we don't get anything like that here, do we?' Jules muttered, her gaze fixed on the TV.

The video was a montage of action from women's matches, and everything looked slick and professional – about a million miles away from Hounslow Harriers. I watched as one player, a woman with her dark hair tied up in a ponytail, took a free kick, and blasted it past the defensive wall into the corner of the net.

'That's Mia Hamm,' Jules told me, as the team celebrated.

We watched the video to the end. Jules was right – it was like a different world. I really envied her having the chance to play in the States. When the American scout Joe had mentioned came to visit, he was bound to be interested in Jules. *And what about me*, whispered a tiny voice at the back of my mind. I pushed it away. It didn't matter one way or the other if the scout was interested in me. I wouldn't be going anywhere.

'So, Jess.' Jules turned the TV off and looked at me. 'When are you going to tell your parents about your game?'

I groaned. 'Oh, I dunno.'

'You can't keep lying to them,' Jules pointed out. 'You're too good—'

'Jules?' Someone was calling, coming up the stairs. 'Sweetheart?'

'It's my mum,' Jules hissed.

I dived across the room, and shoved the shoes into my bag. Then we both sat down on the bed, looking innocent.

'Jules?' Mrs Paxton came into the bedroom, and stopped short. 'Oh, you've got company.'

Mrs Paxton was wearing cut-off jeans and a tight blue shirt with high-heeled white mules and lots of gold jewellery. She looked very glamorous. Her hair was blonde and wavy, and she was beautifully made-up. Her cleavage was a bit over the top, though. Jules had told me that her mum worked in a lingerie shop on Ealing Broadway, and was always trying to get her to wear lacy numbers instead of sports bras. She was always on at poor Jules to be more girly. She just didn't get that Jules wasn't interested.

'Mum, this is Jess,' Jules said.

Mrs Paxton beamed at me. 'Hello, love.' Then she frowned. 'Jess. Is that Indian?'

'It's really Jesminder,' I explained, 'but only my mum calls me that.'

'Jesminder. That's nice. Lovely.' Mrs Paxton nodded encouragingly at me. 'Well, Jesminder, I bet your room at home doesn't look like this – with all these great big butch women on the walls.' And she waved a hand at Jules' posters.

'Mum!' Jules groaned.

Mrs Paxton homed in on me again. 'Jess, I hope you can teach my daughter a bit about your culture, including respecting your elders and the like.'

I tried not to laugh. Beside me, Jules rolled her eyes and pulled a face.

'Cheeky madam,' her mum said fondly. 'You're a lucky girl, aren't you, Jess? I expect your parents will be fixing you up with a nice, handsome doctor soon – a pretty girl like you.'

'Mum!' Jules shrieked. 'Stop embarrassing yourself!'

Mrs Paxton looked hurt. 'I'm just being friendly,

Juliette,' she said. 'You don't mind, do you, Jess, love? 'Course not. Now, are you a friend from school or work?'

I didn't have to reply because Jules did it for me.

'She's a footballer,' she said with a grin. 'Jess is on the team with me.'

Mrs Paxton looked as if Jules had said I was a serial killer or something. She was obviously shocked and disappointed, and her face fell. I was dying to burst out laughing, but I couldn't because it would have been rude. I bit my lip hard, and managed to hold on until Jules had rushed me out of the house after a hasty goodbye. We made it to the 120 bus stop, and then we both collapsed in hysterics, clutching each other for support.

'Did you see her *face*?' Jules giggled.

'*Juliette*,' I snorted, doing a crap imitation of her mum.

'*Jesminder*,' Jules joined in, and we laughed even harder.

I was in a pretty good mood by the time I got home. Even my ankle was feeling better. I bounced in through the door, beaming all over my face – and came to a sudden stop. The first person I saw was

Pinky. She was standing in the kitchen doorway, a hanky clutched in her hand. Dad was standing by the fireplace looking stern, and Mum looked tearful too. Teetu's awful parents were sitting on the sofa, staring at me like I was a piece of dirt on the floor.

'Sats-sri-akal, Uncleji, Auntieji.' I greeted them nervously, wondering what the hell was going on. The atmosphere in the living-room was arctic, and everyone was glaring at *me*, for some reason.

'Look, we're not trying to cause trouble,' Teetu's dad blustered, heaving himself off the sofa. 'We just felt it our duty to tell you. Now it is a matter for your own family.'

Teetu's mum stood up too, her face even grimmer than usual.

'Listen.' Dad came forward, looking upset. 'You know how hard it is for our children here. Sometimes they misjudge things, and try to be too western.'

Teetu's mum looked unconvinced. 'All I know is that children are a map of their parents,' she snapped, hustling her husband towards the front door. 'Sats-sri-akal.'

I stood aside as they went out. What on *earth* was going on?

'You stupid flippin' cow!' Pinky yelled, charging

across the kitchen towards me, as the door clicked shut behind Teets' parents.

'You've ruined your sister's life!' Mum wailed. 'Are you happy now?'

I just stared at them with my mouth open. I didn't have a clue what they were going on about.

'My whole wedding's been called off because of you,' Pinky sobbed.

'*Me!*' I couldn't believe my ears. 'Why?'

'They saw you,' Mum snapped. 'Being . . .' She searched for the right word. '*Filthy* with an English boy!'

'They're lying!' I gasped. 'I wasn't with any English boy.'

'They saw you today at a bus stop kissing him,' Pinky retorted furiously. 'You bitch! Why couldn't you do it in secret like everybody else?'

'Kissing? Me? A boy?' I spluttered. 'You're mad, you're all bloody mad!'

'Jesminder, don't use those swearing words,' Dad said sharply.

Suddenly, I got it. Bus stop. English boy. Trust Teetu's dumb parents to make a mistake like that. The *idiots*.

'I *was* at the 120 bus stop today with my friend

Juliette,' I explained quickly. 'She's a *girl*. And we weren't kissing or anything, for God's sake.' I had to convince them I was telling the truth or I'd never be allowed out of the house again.

Dad pointed at the picture of Guru Nanak on the wall. 'Swear by Babaji,' he said sternly.

'I swear on Babaji's name,' I said quietly.

Everyone was silent, except for Pinky who was sitting on the sofa, sobbing.

'These English girls have such short hair,' Mum muttered, sinking into a chair. 'Sometimes you just can't tell.'

'They must have made a mistake,' Dad agreed.

'That boy's shameless parents are just making an excuse,' Mum went on. 'We were never good enough for them.'

My knees felt wobbly with relief – until Pinky opened her big mouth again.

'No, Mum, it's all *her* fault,' she moaned. 'I bet she was with some dykey girl from her football team. She's still been playing, you know.'

'Pinky!' I hissed.

'She ain't got a job or nothing,' Pinky went on hysterically. 'She's been lying!'

Mum and Dad stared at me, totally shocked. I

groaned. Now I really *was* in for it.

'Oh, God!' Mum wailed dramatically. 'Why did you give me two deceiving daughters? What did I do wrong in my past life?'

Pinky pointed an accusing finger at me. 'She's the one who's ruined *my* life—'

'Be quiet!' Mum broke in crossly. 'Do you think I didn't know you'd been sneaking out with that good-for-nothing Teetu?'

That shut Pinky up. Mum looked from me to Pinky and back again. I knew exactly what she was going to say.

'Well, that's it,' she snapped. 'No more going out for either of you.'

So that was the end of my football career, such as it was. I wasn't allowed out of the house, and I couldn't get to the training sessions. I was gutted, and Pinky was as miserable as I was. The wedding was still off, even though Teetu's parents had been told the truth. Like Mum said, they were using it as an excuse to split Teetu and Pinky up.

I was bored out of my mind. I kept wondering how the other girls were getting on in training, and who'd replace me in the next match of the tournament, which was coming up. And I couldn't get Joe out of my head. Was I ever going to see him again? It didn't seem very likely.

The house was like a morgue. Mum was still mad with both of us, and Dad went around looking upset. He'd taken the fairy lights down from the front of the house, so all our nosy neighbours were gossiping about the wedding not happening. Pinky had taken a sickie from work, and was spending all her time in her room, crying. I was sent upstairs every mealtime to see if she was coming down to eat or not.

'Pinky?' I tapped tentatively on her bedroom door. It was a few days later, and Mum was finally starting to calm down. I'd missed two training sessions by now, and I was wondering what Joe was thinking. Would he be worried? Would he ask Jules where I was? I'd thought about phoning her to tell her what had happened, but I couldn't see any point. It was too painful to be reminded about what I was missing.

'Pinky?' I pushed the door open warily. We hadn't really made up since the row. 'It's dinner-time. Are you coming down?'

Pinky shook her head. She was sitting on her bed, her eyes swollen and red, clutching a wet tissue. She was surrounded by every cuddly toy and giant, schmaltzy card that Teetu had ever bought her.

'Sorry I told them about your football,' she muttered.

'It's OK.' I gave her a hug. 'They'd have found out soon enough. They always do.'

I went back downstairs, feeling better now that Pinky and I were talking again. Mum and Dad were sitting at the table, waiting to start.

'How's your sister?' Mum asked. 'It's time she stopped crying now. She's lucky she found out what a bad mother-in-law she nearly had.'

We all sat there in silence. None of us felt like talking. Just as I leaned over to take a *chapatti*, the doorbell rang.

Before any of us could move, Pinky came thundering down the stairs. 'I'll get it!' she yelled. She was obviously hoping it was Teetu.

Pinky flung the door open eagerly. I turned round to see who it was – and nearly passed out on the spot.

'Hello,' said Joe.

SEVEN

I carried the tray of tea in from the kitchen with shaking hands, hoping no-one would notice the cups rattling in their saucers. There was an awkward silence in the living-room. Dad, Mum and Pinky were sitting staring at Joe, and not in a friendly way. But at least they hadn't kicked him out without hearing what he had to say.

I put the tray down on the coffee table, and handed Joe a cup.

'Thanks, Jess,' he said quietly.

I sat down on a corner of the sofa, stealing a glance at him. It was great to see him again. My heart was thumping and my insides were flipping every time he looked at me. But I had to be careful. Pinky could spot a romance a mile away. If Mum and Dad suspected that I was crazy about my coach, my chances of playing for the team again would be even more microscopic than they were right now.

I wondered if Joe had come just to find out why I hadn't been at training, or if Jules had told him that my parents hadn't known I was playing for the team all this time. Either way, he'd probably guessed the situation by now, based on the dirty looks he was getting.

Joe cleared his throat. 'I'm sorry to barge in on you, Mr and Mrs Bhamra,' he said, 'but I wanted to talk to you in person. I only found out today that you didn't know Jess was playing for our team.'

'No, we didn't,' Mum snapped.

'I apologise.' Joe looked straight at Mum, and I loved him for it. Jules must've told him, so he'd known when he decided to come round here that it was going to be tough. He'd still come though. Oh, I knew it was just because he wanted me back on the team, but it made me feel good. 'If I'd known, I would've encouraged Jess to tell you –' he paused, then went on '– because I believe she's got tremendous potential.'

We all sat there in silence for a few seconds.

'I think we know best our daughter's potential,' Dad said quietly. 'Jess has no time for games. She'll be starting university soon.'

'But playing for the team is an honour,' I blurted out, unable to keep quiet any longer.

Mum glared at me. 'What bigger honour is there than respecting your elders?' she demanded.

Dad looked at Joe. 'Young man, when I was a teenager in Nairobi, I was the best fast bowler in my school,' he said curtly. 'Our team even won the East African cup. But when I came to this country, nothing. I wasn't allowed to play in any team. These bloody *goreh* in their clubhouses laughed at my turban and sent me packing.'

I looked down at the floor. I knew about this because Mum had told me, but Dad had never talked about it before.

'I'm sorry, Mr Bhamra,' Joe began. 'But now—'

'Now what?' Dad broke in. 'None of our boys are in any of the football leagues. And you think they'll let our girls in? I don't want to build up Jesminder's hopes –' he glanced over at me '– she'll only end up disappointed like me.'

'But, Dad, it's all changing now,' I said desperately. 'Look at Nasser Hussain. He's the captain of the England cricket team, and he's Asian.'

'Hussain is a Muslim name,' Mum said sternly. 'Their families are different.'

'Oh, *Mum!*'

It was no use. I could tell that they weren't going to give in. Joe got the message too. A few minutes later, he got up to leave without finishing his tea.

I was determined to grab a quick word with him alone, so I walked out to his car with him. Mum gave me a filthy look, but I didn't care. It would probably be the last time I ever saw him.

'Sorry about that,' I muttered as I pulled the front door shut behind me. 'But thanks for trying.'

Joe shrugged. 'We've been invited to play a match in Germany this Saturday. It's a shame you'll miss it.'

My eyes widened. '*Wow!* Germany? Really?' Then my face fell, as I realised that I had more chance of going to the North Pole.

'I can see what you're up against,' Joe said softly. 'But your parents don't always know what's best for you, Jess.'

I stood staring at him as he turned away and got into his car. My mind was buzzing. *Your parents don't always know what's best for you . . .*

Joe was right.

In this case, they didn't.

'OK, you know what to do, yeah?' Pinky said impatiently, as she scorched down the road towards the club.

'Yeah, call them twice a day,' I replied, picking

up her mobile. 'They won't be able to tell I'm in Germany, will they?'

Pinky shook her head. 'Trust me, I'm an expert at this.' She swung the car into the club car park. 'Look, there's your team.'

The girls were all sitting in the minibus, and Joe was just climbing inside. He was pulling the door shut when he spotted the car.

I jumped out, grabbing my bag. 'My sister's covering for me,' I said breathlessly. 'We're supposed to be staying at our cousin's in Croydon.'

Joe smiled at me. 'I didn't hear that.'

I rushed on to the bus, and all the girls cheered. I made my way over to Jules, who was sitting on her own.

'I knew you'd come,' she said with a huge grin. 'I even saved a seat for you.'

'I wouldn't have missed it for anything.' I grinned back at her, pushing the fact that I was deceiving my parents to the back of my mind. I was going to enjoy myself, whatever happened.

Things started off brilliantly. The plane journey was a laugh, and I even enjoyed the plastic meal we were served by the stewardesses. When we arrived in Hamburg, we were whisked out of the airport and on to a luxury bus for the short drive to our hotel. Jules and I were sharing a room, but we hardly had time to unpack before we were off for a river-boat trip around the city.

'Isn't this fab?' Jules yelled in my ear, as the boat sailed along one of the many canals. I nodded. Hamburg was huge, a real mixture of old and new, with churches and museums right alongside big new shopping centres.

'Come on, Jess.' Jules whipped her camera out of her bag. 'Say "cheese"!'

'What do you want a picture of *me* for?' I laughed, doing a mock-sexy pout. I was playing to the camera a bit because I knew that Joe was looking at me. But it was liberating to know that no-one was going to see me and rush to tell Mum and Dad that I wasn't behaving myself properly.

The match against the German team was in the evening, so we headed back to the hotel for lunch and a rest before we went over to the club. We were all up for the game massively. Even though it was a friendly, we were determined to win. I couldn't wait to get out on to the pitch – though there was a secret worry niggling away at the back of my mind. I'd missed several training sessions, and I hadn't even been playing in the park with the lads like I used to. What if I wasn't fit enough for a ninety-minute game?

The German club was amazing. I reckon the German girls would have gone on strike if they'd had the same facilities we were expected to put up with at the Harriers. As I stood on the pitch that evening, waiting for Mel and the German captain to choose halves, I stared round at the immaculate green grass, the huge, comfortable stands filled with people, the state-of-the-art floodlights and the electronic scoreboard. This was easily the biggest crowd I'd ever played in front of. I was desperate to do well.

The ref blew his whistle, and the first half began. The German team were no pushover. They obviously weren't considering the game as just a friendly either, and they were pretty physical. I got a bit frustrated after forty-five minutes when all my runs and attempts to set something up with Jules were blocked. At the half-time whistle, we'd had one shot at goal, a header from Mel, and that was all.

'Don't lose heart,' Joe said urgently to us in the changing-room. 'We're blocking them just as efficiently at our end. It's going to be a question of which side can hold out the longest. Don't give up.'

I felt OK as we ran out for the second half. All my fears about not being fit enough seemed to be unfounded. But as the deadlock continued for the next twenty minutes, I began to wheeze a bit. My pace started to drop, and I was having to push myself hard to keep up with the flow of play.

Suddenly a shout from behind startled me. 'Jess! Mark her!' Mel yelled.

With a sinking heart, I realised that my opponent had got away from me, and was dribbling towards the penalty area, unmarked. I chased after her, but couldn't catch her up. She banged the ball into the net past Charlie, and we were one-nil down.

It was all my fault, I thought gloomily as the German team celebrated. Mel saw my face and came over to put her arm round me. 'Don't worry, Jess,' she said. 'These things happen.'

Yeah, but it wouldn't have happened if I was fit enough, I thought silently. It wasn't fair on the rest of the team. I had to make it up to them somehow.

The match was nearly over and I was almost on my last legs, when I saw a chance. I picked the ball up from Sally, and, as if by magic, a gap suddenly opened up in front of me. I got my second wind, and headed for the German penalty area.

'Jess!' I could hear Jules shrieking as she ran alongside me. *'Pass!'*

I glanced up and hit the ball forward into space. Jules ran on to it, picked it up and thumped the ball into the net. It was just as good as Beckham's last-minute goal against Greece. I almost collapsed with relief.

Jules cartwheeled over to me and I jumped on her, followed by the rest of the team. We were all screaming with joy. The ref had to break it up and hustle us back to the centre circle, but two minutes after we kicked off, he blew the whistle for full-time. A draw.

'Penalties,' Jules said, with a wide smile on her face. 'Let's stuff 'em, girls.'

Although it wasn't usual to finish a friendly with penalties, both sides had decided that it would be a nice idea. Now, with my legs wobbling dangerously underneath me, I wasn't so sure. I hung back as Joe came on to the pitch to give us a quick pep talk. Maybe he wouldn't choose me.

'OK, Jules, you go first,' Joe said briskly. 'Then Mel, Tina, Hannah and –' he turned to me '– Jess.'

I tried not to look relieved that I was last. With any luck I wouldn't have to take my turn, if the match was decided before that.

The Germans went first, and scored. So did Jules, with a cracking shot that nearly broke through the net. The Germans scored again. So did Mel. After a third German goal, Tina was looking nervous, but she was lucky because her shot went in off the post.

My stomach was turning over and over as Hannah stepped up to take our fourth penalty. The Germans hadn't missed one yet. If Hannah scored, it would be all down to the last German penalty-taker – and me.

Hannah sent the goalie the wrong way and rolled the ball smoothly into the left-hand corner of the net. I tried to take deep breaths to calm myself down. If the next German player scored, I'd have to take my turn. I closed my eyes, willing her to fail.

A loud roar around the stadium told me that she'd scored. The ref beckoned to me, and I trudged over to place the ball on the spot. I was incredibly tired, and my legs felt like they were made of lead. Behind me I could hear the girls yelling encouragement.

'Come on, Jess!' That was Jules. 'You can do this.'

I made a superhuman effort and ran towards the

ball, but even as I hit it, I knew it wasn't right. I groaned as the ball hit the crossbar and ricocheted into the crowd. Now I knew exactly how Gareth Southgate, David Batty and all those other players who'd missed penalties for England felt. Like someone had grabbed hold of my insides and ripped them out. Gutted, in other words.

EIGHT

'Yeah, Mum, I'm fine,' I said impatiently. I was standing in our bathroom back at the hotel, watching Jules doing her hair. 'I'm fine, Pinky's fine. We're all cooking – um – pasta. I'd better go, Pinky's burning it. Say hi to Dad. OK, bye, Mum.'

I finally got her off the phone, and switched off the mobile with a sigh of relief. I hadn't really felt like calling home after what had happened. I'd wanted to crawl into bed, pull the covers over me and stay there for a week. Joe had told me not to worry about it, but I knew he was just being nice.

'Come on,' Jules said. 'You'd better start getting ready.'

Looking grumpy, I sat down on my bed, and began pulling T-shirts out of my bag. 'I didn't bring anything for a club,' I said sulkily. 'I didn't know they'd want to take us out. I bet it's to gloat.'

Jules ignored me. She picked up the phone, and dialled a number. 'Mel, we need some help,' she said before replacing the receiver.

'What're you doing?' I demanded.

'You're going to get a makeover,' Jules said with a grin.

'What?' I said. 'I don't *need* a makeover!'

Jules ignored me. Five minutes later there was a knock at the door. Jules opened it, and there was Mel with her arms full of make-up and clothes.

'Let's get to work,' she said to Jules, ignoring my protests.

Half an hour later I didn't even recognise myself when I looked in the mirror. I was wearing make-up for the first time in my life. I'd never bothered before, even when Pinky had offered to lend me hers. Mel had brought her curling-tongs and waved my hair, which I wore loose. Jules had lent me a tight skirt and a shiny black top which looked quite normal from the front, but which was held together with minuscule strips of material at the back. I was showing a lot of skin. What if the strips tore and the top fell straight off me?

We went down to reception to meet the others, me walking really carefully in the high-heeled, strappy sandals that Mel had lent me. We spotted them out in the street looking for taxis and went to join them. I felt strangely shy as I pushed my way through the revolving doors. What would Joe think of my new look?

I don't want to sound big-headed but I think it would be fair to say that his eyes almost fell out of his head when he saw me. The other girls were startled too, but then they started cheering.

'Does she look good or what?' Mel asked proudly. 'Yeah, she looks good!'

Joe stared at me for a few seconds more, then dragged his gaze away. 'Come on, let's get a taxi,' he said.

I smiled to myself. Maybe, just maybe, there *was* something between us. Yeah, yeah, I knew that nothing could ever come of it. But here I was in a strange city miles from home, and looking good. I felt like a different person, and I was going to make the most of it.

We piled into three or four taxis, and headed off for the club. When we got there, I celebrated the new me by ordering a glass of wine. By the time I was on my second glass, I was feeling – not pissed exactly, but pretty relaxed. Jules was sitting chatting to me and some of the other players. She'd been on the dance-floor for some of the time, along with the rest of our team and the German players, but I hadn't joined them. I was a bit nervous about breaking an ankle in Mel's heels. We were laughing and joking around, but all the time I was conscious of Joe sitting at the neighbouring table. He was talking to the German coach, but every now and then he'd glance over at us.

'Jess,' Jules bawled in my ear over the music, 'I'm going to ask Joe to dance.'

I watched as she made her way over. The German coach had gone to the bar, leaving Joe on his own. Jules sat down next to him, and started flirting wildly. I couldn't hear her, but I could tell. And I felt jealous. I decided to join them, so I went over and sat down on Joe's other side. I didn't see why Jules should have everything her own way.

'Come on, dance with me,' Jules was saying, trying to drag Joe to his feet. He shook his head firmly. 'Oh, honestly, Joe – you're such a wuss!'

'I'm sorry I missed that penalty, coach,' I said, looking at him over the top of my wine glass. Maybe it was about time I started to learn to flirt too.

'It's OK,' Joe said with a grin. 'Losing to the Jerries on penalties comes naturally to you English. You're part of a tradition now!'

'Enough about football.' Jules grabbed his hand. 'Come on, you're dancing with me.'

'No,' Joe repeated.

'Come on, I'm not taking no for an answer!'

Joe finally shrugged and gave in. I watched them move on to the dance floor, wishing I had some of Jules' confidence. I *thought* Joe fancied me. But I didn't have the nerve to do anything about it.

Carrying my glass of wine, I made my way across the crowded dance floor towards some of our players. As I was standing chatting to them, someone came up behind me.

'Come on, you're dancing with us,' Joe said in my ear.

I started to shake my head, but he ignored me, took my hand and led me over to Jules. For a few moments we danced together with Joe holding both our hands. Jules looked a bit put out, but she didn't say anything.

Suddenly though, I began to feel dizzy. The club started to spin. I put my hand to my head, and blinked a few times to try to clear my vision, but now my stomach was churning and I felt sick. Quickly I turned and made my way unsteadily towards the back doors of the club, which were open on to the street. I needed some fresh air.

'Oh!' I stumbled as I got outside, and someone grabbed my arm.

'Careful.' It was Joe. I hadn't realised that he'd followed me. 'Are you all right?'

'Oh, God,' I muttered, feeling really sick now. 'I only had a couple of glasses of wine.' I groaned. 'Oh, my head. It's too smoky in there.'

Joe put his arm round me and helped me over to a nearby wall. I leaned against him, partly because my legs felt like jelly, and partly because I enjoyed being near him. We stood there in silence for a moment, then I looked up at him.

'That was so brilliant, the way you came to my house.' My heart thudded loudly as he smiled at me and stroked my hair. 'You were brave enough to face my mum. Your dad can't be as mad as *her*!'

'Your mum was a barrel of laughs compared to my dad,' Joe replied softly. 'I don't need to be close to my family, Jess. You don't have to feel sorry for me.'

I smiled back at him. I knew what I wanted to do next. I wanted to kiss him, and nothing was going to stop me . . .

I leaned forwards, raising my face to him. Joe

hesitated for a second, then he leaned towards me too.

'You bitch!'

I gasped and spun round – just in time to see the hurt look on Jules' face as she disappeared back into the club.

It was a disaster. But that wasn't the end of it. Jules refused to talk to me and moved out to spend our last night in Mel's room. She wouldn't talk to me the next day on the journey home either, and she made sure she sat by someone else on the bus to the airport and during the flight.

I tried to apologise to her. I blamed my behaviour on the glasses of wine that I'd drunk, saying that I'd never have done anything like that if I hadn't been pissed. But deep down, I kept asking myself – *would* I have tried to kiss Joe even if I was stone-cold sober? I didn't know. And Jules seemed to guess that I wasn't being straight with her, which was why she was so furious with me.

I hadn't spoken to Joe either. We'd avoided each other, both us of hanging out with other girls in the team to make sure we weren't left alone together. I wondered if he regretted what had nearly happened between us. I couldn't tell.

The awkwardness between Jules, Joe and me affected the whole team, and we sat on the minibus home in gloomy silence. I'd made sure I was sitting near Jules, even though she didn't look at me once during the journey, or speak to me. I wanted to try and corner her when the minibus stopped, and see if I could talk to her. We had to get this sorted out. One, because we were good mates and I didn't want to lose her friendship. And two, because we couldn't play together properly and keep up our partnership on the pitch if we were at each other's throats.

But when the minibus stopped, Jules was first out of her seat. She grabbed her bag, and ran for it. I jumped up and pushed my way to the front of the bus.

'Jules!'

It was too late. She'd gone. I stared after her, wondering how I was ever going to get her to listen to me. Still, I'd see her at the next training session.

Mel was getting off the bus behind me. 'All right, Jess?' she asked.

I didn't answer.

'Who are they?' Mel asked curiously, pointing across the car park.

I'd already seen them myself. Mum, Dad and Pinky were standing by the car, staring at me. Oh hell.

NINE

Mum and Dad didn't shout. They didn't yell and they didn't have a go at me. We got quietly into the car, and Mum started crying. I felt like a traitor for betraying their trust in me.

We arrived home, and my parents went straight upstairs without speaking. I felt sick, and my insides were knotted up with tension. This was worse than being yelled at.

'How did they find out?' I asked Pinky in a low voice.

'Dad saw a picture of your team in the paper,' she replied listlessly. 'And there was an article about your Hamburg trip. He guessed.' She looked washed-out, and she had dark circles under her eyes. She wasn't even wearing any make-up, which was like going out without any clothes on for my sister. I felt really sorry for her. This business with Teetu was still getting to her, and now I'd dragged her into even more trouble.

'What happened?'

'They turned up in Croydon and brought me

home,' Pinky replied, then she turned away and trudged upstairs.

I watched her go. I knew that this was finally *it*. I had to make my mind up what I was going to do. If I carried on the way I was, I was going to keep hurting my parents. They'd looked shell-shocked when they'd picked me up after the trip, as if they couldn't believe what I'd done and didn't know how to handle it. If I kept on playing, we were going to fall out big-time. Was that what I really wanted?

And then there was Joe . . .

I went upstairs. I could still hear the murmur of my parents' voices from behind closed doors. I could guess what they were saying.

'Pinky?' I went into my sister's bedroom. She was sitting on the bed, looking miserable, and she didn't seem too pleased to see me. But I had something to ask her.

'Pinks, how do you know Teets is the one?' I asked tentatively.

My sister's face softened. 'I just know,' she said quietly. 'When you're in love you'd do anything to be with that person . . .'

I was silent for a moment, wondering if that was how I felt about Joe.

'Do you think Mum and Dad would still speak to me if I ever brought home a *gora*?' I blurted out.

Pinky was on to me like a shot. 'Who're you talking about?'

'No-one.' I tried to look innocent. 'I'm just saying.'

'It's that coach bloke, isn't it?' Pinky looked scandalised. 'I *knew* something was going on when he turned up here!'

So she *had* noticed.

'Nothing's happened,' I said quickly.

Pinky gave me a warning look. 'Well, make sure it doesn't, all right?'

I bit my lip. If Pinky didn't think it could work, what chance did I have?

'Look, Jess, you can marry anyone you want,' my sister went on in a more reasonable voice. 'It's fine at first when you're in love and all that.' She shrugged her shoulders. 'But do you *really* want to be the one everyone stares at, at every family do, because you're married to an English bloke?'

'He's Irish,' I said sadly. I knew that there was a lot of truth in what she said, however much I didn't want to hear it.

'Well, they all look the bloody same to them,' Pinky pointed out. 'Why go to so much grief when there are so many good-looking Indian guys around? It's not like before, Jess. They wear good clothes now, they've got flashy jobs. They even know how to cook and wash up.' She glanced sideways at me. 'What about Tony? He's been mad on you for ages.'

I nodded. She hadn't given me the advice I'd wanted to hear. But then, I hadn't expected her to. Nobody understood. I couldn't even talk to my favourite poster of Beckham any more. I had just one question spinning round and round in my mind. *What was I going to do?* Whatever I decided, someone was going to get hurt . . .

I walked up to the clubhouse, and peered nervously through the open door. I was looking for Joe, and I didn't have much time. Mum had let me out of the house reluctantly when I told her I needed to go to the library. But she'd expect me back in an hour or two, and I had somewhere else I needed to go after I'd seen Joe.

Joe was in the clubhouse, standing at the bar. He was talking to two older men, one of whom I recognised as the chairman of the club. I thought the other guy might be the secretary. I watched as they shook hands with Joe and went off through the other door. I moved away, loosened my ponytail and let my hair fall around my shoulders. I wanted to look good for him, although I was wearing my usual trackies and sweat-top. Don't tell me. Stupid, I know.

Joe had spotted me, and he walked over, his expression unreadable. I couldn't tell if he was embarrassed, glad to see me or wished I was ten thousand miles away.

'Hi,' I said, trying to avoid his eyes.

'Hi.'

There was an awkward silence.

'Was that the club chairman?' I asked. Anything to put off what I was about to tell him.

'Yeah.' Joe looked down at his feet. 'They've told me they're considering me for assistant coach to the men's side next year.'

'That's great.' I honestly did feel pleased for him. He'd worked hard for this chance. 'Congratulations.'

'I probably won't get it,' Joe said quietly. 'It's better not to count on anything.'

Another silence.

'Well, you deserve it,' I said. I took a deep breath and groped for the right words. 'Look, I'm sorry about—'

'I've already forgotten it,' Joe jumped in.

'Yeah, good.' I cleared my throat. 'Me too.'

'Your mum and dad didn't look too pleased yesterday,' Joe said. Understatement of the millennium, I thought. 'I suppose you've come to tell me you're off the team.'

I hung my head. That was exactly why I was there. The semi-final was coming up on Sunday, and I was giving Joe plenty of notice so that he could sort out a replacement. It had all seemed so simple earlier that morning, but now I was torn in two again.

'It's not fair,' I mumbled. 'I feel like I'm either going to let the team down or really piss my parents off. I don't want to upset *anyone*.'

Joe shook his head. 'Why are they so frightened to let you play?' he asked, looking genuinely puzzled.

'They want to protect me,' I said.

'From what?'

I raised my head and looked pointedly at him. We both blushed.

'This is taking me away from everything they know,' I explained.

Joe looked frustrated. I didn't blame him; I felt the same way myself. 'Whose life are you living, Jess? If you try pleasing them forever, you're going to end up blaming them.'

'What, like you?' The words were out of my mouth before I could stop them.

Joe looked away from me.

'Sorry—' I began.

'No, you're right,' Joe interrupted me. 'I stopped talking to my dad because we had nothing to talk about. After my injury, I spent a year trying to forget about the game, but I couldn't.'

'But I can't just stop talking to them like you,' I muttered. My family irritated the hell out of me sometimes, but they were still my family. I couldn't just do what *I* wanted and leave them behind.

'I don't talk to my dad because I know what he'd say,' Joe said abruptly. 'He'd laugh himself stupid if he found out I was coaching girls.'

'How do you *know* that?' I argued. 'How do you know that he wouldn't be proud that you just didn't give up?'

Joe didn't look very convinced. Then he looked me straight in the eye. 'Like you're just giving up?'

His words stung, but I just shook my head dully. He didn't understand.

* * *

'Oh, hello.' Mrs Paxton beamed at me, opening the front door wider. 'It's Jasvinder, isn't it?'

'Jesminder,' I corrected her. I was taking a chance coming to see Jules, but I had to make her listen to me. Even if I was off the team, I didn't want her to hate me.

'Oh, yes, Jesminder,' Mrs Paxton repeated. 'I'm sorry. Come in, dear.' I stepped into the hall. 'Jules is in her bedroom. I'll just show you up there.'

I followed Mrs Paxton up the stairs. Even though it was early in the morning, she was all tarted up in a floral skirt, low-cut T-shirt, high heels and loads of make-up. She went ahead of me, trailing perfume, and opened Jules' bedroom door.

'Darling – oh, are you still not up?' She sounded concerned. 'Guess who's come to see you?'

I followed Mrs Paxton into the room just in time to see Jules pull herself up from her pillows. She gave me an icy glare and didn't say a word.

'It's your Indian friend from football,' her mum went on, bustling across the room to open the curtains. 'Oh, Jules has been ever so down since you lost in Germany. Maybe you can cheer her up, though.'

At the moment it looked like the only thing that

would cheer Jules up was murdering me, so I didn't reply.

Mrs Paxton came over to stand next to me and put her hand on my shoulder. 'Did you want a cup of tea, Jess?' she asked. 'And I've just made some cheese straws, with real Gruyère.'

'No, it's all right, Mum,' Jules snapped. 'Jess won't be staying long.'

'Oh.' Her mum looked uncertainly from Jules to me. I think she'd finally sussed that there was something major going on. 'Well, just shout down the stairs if there's anything you two fancy,' she said, going over to the door as slowly as she could. I got the feeling she was dying to know what was happening, but couldn't quite bring herself to ask.

I stood there uncomfortably until I heard Mrs Paxton going down the stairs. She'd looked so curious, I wouldn't have put it past her to stand outside the door, trying to get an earful. 'Look, Jules,' I began. That was when I noticed the photo of Joe and Jules lying crumpled on top of the wastebasket. 'I feel really bad about what happened.'

'Well, you should,' Jules retorted bitterly.

'I'm sorry.' I tried again. 'I don't want you to be in a strop with me.'

'I am NOT in a strop!' Jules hissed.

'It was a mistake,' I gabbled. 'I didn't know what I was doing.'

Jules looked so hurt I felt sick. 'I can't *believe* you kissed him!' she burst out.

I was gobsmacked. 'I didn't—'

'Yeah, right,' Jules said scornfully. 'I know what I saw. You *knew* he was off-limits.'

I didn't know what to say. I hadn't realised that she thought I'd *actually* kissed Joe. But God, what did it matter? There was that evil little voice at the back of my mind, sticking its nose in again. I *would've* kissed him if Jules hadn't turned up . . .

'Don't pretend to be so innocent!' Jules flared. 'You knew exactly how I felt about him!'

'But you told me you didn't like him,' I defended myself. 'And now you're acting like you're in love with him!'

Jules didn't answer. She rolled over in bed, staring at the wall so that I couldn't see her face. I felt helpless.

'So that's it?' I asked. My voice was shaking, and I didn't even try to hide it.

'That's it.' Jules pulled the duvet over her head and lay very still.

Biting my lip, I ran out of the bedroom and down the stairs. Mrs Paxton was standing at the bottom with a tea tray in her hands. I didn't want her to see how upset I was, so I slipped past her and made for the front door.

I pulled it open. Jules' dad was outside, just about to put his key in the lock, and he looked surprised to see me. I wondered if Jules had told him what had happened. I knew that she was close to her dad because he always stood up for her against her mum when she was having a go about Jules playing football.

'Bye,' I mumbled, glancing round at Mrs Paxton.

She didn't answer me. She looked pretty upset herself, for some reason. God knows why. But she couldn't be half as upset as I was. My whole life was falling to bits around me, and I didn't have a clue what to do about it.

TEN

'Tony, do you fancy me?' I asked abruptly.

Tony looked pretty taken aback. We were sitting in the bandstand in the park watching the other boys playing football and, up until a few seconds ago, we'd been talking about what a prat Taz could be. My sudden change of subject had gobsmacked him completely. He stared at me as if I'd suddenly grown two heads or something.

'*Do* you fancy me, Tony?' I repeated impatiently. I was trying to think of something I could do to get Joe out of my head. Going out with someone else was my best idea so far.

'I like you, yeah,' Tony said cautiously, but he didn't sound over-enthusiastic. But then again, neither was I.

'Well, good,' I said briskly. 'Maybe we can go out together then, yeah?'

Tony laughed nervously. He was hardly jumping at the chance I was offering him, which certainly wasn't doing a whole lot for my ego. 'Jess, what's going on?'

'I'm sorry, Tony,' I mumbled. 'I just think I need an Indian boyfriend . . .'

'What *is* going on, Jess?' Tony asked again, looking even more confused. 'You're acting all weird.'

'Sorry.' I hesitated, wondering how much to tell him. 'You know my coach?'

Tony nodded.

'Well, I – I nearly kissed him in Germany,' I confessed, my face burning with embarrassment.

Tony burst out laughing. 'Wow!' he exclaimed. 'So *that's* why you need an Indian boyfriend?'

'Well, Jules likes him too, and now she hates me,' I finished off gloomily.

'Look, Jess, you can't plan who you fall for,' Tony pointed out. 'It just happens. Look at . . .' He frowned for a minute, thinking. 'Posh and Becks!'

I grinned. 'Beckham is the *best*.'

'I really like Beckham too,' Tony agreed.

'Of course you do,' I said. 'No-one can cross a ball or bend it like Beckham.'

Tony was staring at me in a very strange way. 'No, Jess,' he said gently. 'I *really* like Beckham.'

For a second or two I didn't understand what he meant. Then, finally, I sussed exactly what he was saying, and my eyes opened wide.

'What? You mean . . . ?' I couldn't quite get the words out.

Tony nodded.

'But you're Indian!' I gasped. Which was probably the least helpful thing I could have come up with.

'I haven't told anyone yet,' Tony said quickly. 'Only you.'

I sat there in shock. Tony was *gay*? We'd been mates for years, and I'd never noticed a thing. Then I couldn't help smiling as something suddenly struck me. 'God, what's your mum going to say?'

Tony shrugged, and I finally began to take in what all this meant for him. Gays weren't part of Indian culture. Everyone pretended they just didn't exist. What the hell was Tony going to do? At some point in his life, he was going to have to make some difficult choices. I stared at him as if I was seeing him properly for the very first time, knowing that he was going to have the same problems I was having with *my* parents if he wanted to live his own life. Choosing a different lifestyle to the one everyone expected you to have meant big trouble. Suddenly, I didn't feel quite so alone.

'My sister thinks you're mad about me,' I teased him.

'I am,' Tony replied. 'I just don't want to marry you.'

He got up and walked across to the other side of the bandstand. I followed him, and we stood watching Taz and the others playing footie for a few minutes.

I grinned. 'I wonder what all those tossers would say if they knew.'

Tony looked alarmed. 'Jess, you're not going to tell anyone?'

'Of course not,' I said quickly. 'It's OK, Tony. I mean, it's OK with me . . .'

'Well, you fancying your *gora* coach is OK with *me*,' Tony said solemnly. 'Besides, he's kind of fit!'

We both burst out laughing. Maybe I *could* cope. After all, I wasn't the only person in the world who had problems . . .

I sneezed really convincingly into my hanky and wiped my nose. Mum looked anxiously at me, as she went over to the front door with Dad.

'Go back to bed, Jessie,' she ordered me. 'We'll see you later.'

I nodded, pulling my dressing-gown around me tightly.

'Listen, you've got to be back by three o'clock,' Pinky whispered in my ear. 'I won't be able to keep them at the temple all afternoon.'

I nodded. 'I owe you big-time, Pinks.'

It was Sunday, the day of the semi-final, and I'd finally made up my mind that I was going to play. I didn't want to upset Mum and Dad, but how could I possibly keep away? I'd worked my butt off to help the team get through to the semis – I couldn't miss out now. I didn't know what was going to happen in the future. I didn't even know if I'd be playing again after today. But I was determined that I wasn't going to miss what might be my last chance to turn out for the Harriers.

I stood waving in the doorway, as Dad manoeuvred the car off the drive.

'Bring me lots of *langar*,' I called.

'Chi!' Mum snorted through the open window. 'We're going to pray to God to give you both sense, not bring back lots of food for you.'

I watched the car drive off, then dashed inside, whipping off my dressing-gown. I already had my kit on underneath because the match would be about to start by the time I got there. I was cutting it pretty fine, I thought, glancing at the clock as I pulled on my boots. I'd have to run all the way. I let myself out of the front door, trying not to look at the picture of Guru Nanak on the wall. Why did I always have to feel guilty whenever I stood up for myself and made a decision I thought was right, I asked myself crossly.

I hadn't told Joe or any of the Harriers that I was coming. As I legged it down the street towards the ground, an unpleasant thought struck me. Maybe Joe would be annoyed with me for messing the team around. After all, he needed players he could rely on. I'd told him at the clubhouse that I was off the team – well, that I almost certainly wouldn't be turning up for the semi-final. Maybe he'd get tired of me changing my mind all the time.

I needn't have worried. By the time I arrived, both teams were already out on the pitch warming up. Joe spotted me, and I saw his face light up. But all he said was, 'So you made it, Bhamra. Get yourself out on to the pitch right away.'

I jogged out towards the centre circle, feeling all fired up as if I could run a marathon. There was a buzz from the crowd, which was much bigger than we were normally used to. It made the whole occasion feel much more special. I glanced round the seats, trying to spot Tony, who was coming to give us some support. He was sitting about halfway up the stand, and I was surprised to see that Taz, Sonny and some of the other lads were with him. They'd probably come to eye up the players, I thought with a grin. I noticed Jules' dad too, although Mrs Paxton wasn't there.

'Good to see you, Jess,' Mel called as I joined the rest of the team. I grinned at her, and looked around for Jules. She was over the other side of the field, pretending that she hadn't noticed me and therefore couldn't possibly be ignoring me. As I warmed up I kept glancing over at her nervously. What was going to happen to our goal-scoring partnership if she kept sulking once the match started? The whole team would suffer. I didn't think Jules would be that petty, but I couldn't be sure. She *was* as mad as hell with me.

'Come on, the Harriers!' roared the crowd, as the ref blew the whistle for the first half. Well, maybe *roared* is exaggerating a bit. There weren't enough of them for that. But at least they were cheering us on.

The first half was a disaster. Our team was jittery and tense, and we couldn't seem to string more than two passes together. It could just have been nerves because we were playing in the semi-final, but I couldn't help thinking that maybe it was because the others were affected by the atmosphere between me and Jules. I was trying to avoid passing to her because I didn't know how she was going to react, and I think she was doing the same. I had another problem too. My marker, a girl called Zoe Turner, was a lot bigger than me, and she was needling me constantly, stepping on my heels, nudging me in the back and generally getting right up my nose. I'd got away from her a few times because I was faster, but she'd retaliated by marking me extra-close when she caught up with me. The ref hadn't noticed all the shirt-tugging, kicking and nudges, and it was starting to get on my nerves.

Five minutes before half-time, everything went wrong. Millwall's centre-forward suddenly broke free, cutting a trail through the middle of the pitch and leaving our defence for dead.

'Wake up, Harriers!' Joe yelled from the touchline, as our defenders chased helplessly after the other girl. 'It's not half-time yet! Get after her!'

They'd have needed a car to catch her, I thought gloomily, as Charlie came out of the goal to try to block the girl's shot. It was no good. The player had got the scent of victory, and she wasn't going to let it get away. She banged the ball into the back of the net and Millwall celebrated loudly, while we just stood around looking at each other in disgust.

Back in the dressing-room, a steely-eyed Joe had a go at us.

'I don't expect to see gaps at the back that you could drive a bus through,' he snapped, eyeballing the defenders. 'Stop overplaying the off-side rule – they're getting more out of it than you are.' He turned to me, then his gaze moved to Jules, who'd carefully chosen a seat as far away from me as possible. 'Bhamra, Paxton, I want you to start playing as if you're on the same team.' His eyes raked over both of us. 'You *are* on the same team, aren't you?'

We both nodded. As we filed out for the second half, I stole a glance at Jules. Neither of us had played half as well as we could have done. Although we were good individual players, things really started to happen when our partnership was working. It was up to us to turn this game around.

The second half started off fast and furious. Millwall had decided that the best way to crush us completely was to get another goal as fast as they could. Because they were pushing forward, they kept leaving gaps at the back and several times both Jules and I managed to make runs into their penalty area.

Our breakthrough came in the fifty-sixth minute. I'd left Zoe Turner behind yet again, and was thundering down the touchline towards Millwall's goal. I could see Jules in the penalty area, watching me. I turned smoothly on the ball and crossed it straight towards her.

Jules jumped up, high above all the other players, and headed the ball into the net. We'd equalised!

The other Harriers rushed over to Jules and leapt on her. Jules didn't even look at me so I stayed well away from the celebrations, and applauded politely. I felt a bit left out, but I reckoned that if I *had* gone over and put my arm round Jules, she'd have punched me on the nose. I was pretty sure that no-one had ever been sent off for attacking one of their own team, but there was always a first time.

Now that Jules had scored, *I* wanted a goal too. It was getting more difficult for me to dodge Turner because she was becoming frustrated and trying every trick in the book to stop me. She was hassling me again as I ran into the box, keeping an eye on Jules dribbling the ball down the wing. Jules was too far away to take a shot herself, but I was perfectly placed, if I could just get away from my opponent.

The Millwall defenders were expecting a high cross into the box, but Jules outfoxed them. Instead, she hit a waist-high cross straight towards me. I didn't have time to bring the ball down because Turner was so close to me. So I trapped the ball neatly on my thigh, and fired in a volley. The Millwall goalie had no chance, and the crowd went mad as the ball flew into the net.

'YES!' I ran down the pitch, my arms outstretched, wheeling like a plane. The other girls ran after me, whooping and cheering, and we had a massive team hug. Except Jules, who stayed over the other side of the pitch, applauding politely. Just like I'd done when she'd scored.

I was flying now, and nothing and nobody could stop me. Ten minutes later, I picked up the ball from Mel, and dashed forward down the middle of the pitch. I had the goal in my sights again.

Suddenly my stomach lurched as I was yanked roughly backwards. Someone had grabbed hold of my shirt, and they weren't letting go. I staggered and spun round, losing my balance and falling on to the grass. 'What the hell are you playing at?' I yelled at Zoe Turner, as the ref came running over.

Turner glared at me. 'What's the matter, Paki?' she sneered.

I saw all shades of red. I jumped to my feet, boiling with rage, and ran at her. I gave her a hard shove with both my hands, which sent her flying, and she ended up sprawling on the grass. The Millwall team screeched with rage and began yelling at the ref to sort it out.

The ref was blowing his whistle, looking stern, and Mel was in the thick of things, trying to calm me, the ref and everyone else down. But I was too angry to care. I'd been called names before, and I'd always stood up for myself. But somehow I'd never expected it to happen to me *here*. How naive could you get?

The ref was waving Mel, Tina and some of our other players away. 'Number Seven,' he called sternly. 'Come here.'

I walked over to him, still furious and upset. I thought I was just going to get booked – until I saw the red card in his hand.

'You're sending me *off*?' I gasped.

The crowd were whistling and shouting. I could even hear a few boos as I trudged off the pitch. Jules was watching me, straight-faced. She didn't look pleased or sympathetic or anything. I didn't dare look at Joe, I just made my way to the changing-room.

'You prat,' I told myself angrily. 'You shouldn't have let her get up your nose. You should just have ignored her. After all, lots of black players in the football league have to put up with that, and worse, every week.' But *why* did we have to put up with it, I argued silently. It wasn't right. It wasn't fair. And how come *I* was the one who got sent off? Was shoving someone worse than racist abuse? I didn't think so.

I was showered and changed by the time the match finished. The rest of the Harriers rushed in singing *We Are the Champions*, so I knew we'd won. I was mightily relieved. If they'd lost through being one girl down, I'd have felt horribly guilty.

I got some smiles and sympathetic looks, and Charlie ruffled my hair, but I couldn't say anything. Then I stiffened as Joe walked in.

'Well done,' he yelled over all the excited chatter. 'You were excellent!' Then he spotted me sitting forlornly on the bench, and his face changed. He strode over to me. 'What the hell's wrong with you, Bhamra?' he shouted. I jumped, and everyone else stopped talking to listen. 'I don't want to see anything like that from you again, do you hear me? We're lucky they're not suspending players from this tournament.'

He turned away, dismissing me, and I felt tears pricking at my eyelids. Where did he get off, shouting at me like that? 'Right, we've got QPR in the final,' Joe went on. 'Give yourself three cheers – hip hip . . .'

I didn't join in the cheering. I was shaking with anger, as well as from the effort of trying not to cry. When Joe walked out of the clubhouse, I ran straight after him.

'Why did you yell at me like that?' I demanded aggressively, as I caught up with him. 'You know that ref was out of order!'

'Jess,' Joe said in a much more reasonable voice, 'you could have cost us the tournament.'

'But it wasn't my fault,' I said, my voice quivering. 'You didn't have to shout at me.'

'I'm your coach, Jess,' Joe pointed out. 'I have to treat you the same as everyone else. Look, I saw her foul you. You just overreacted, that's all.'

This time I started to cry. I couldn't help it. 'That's *not* all,' I sobbed. 'She called me a Paki. But I guess you wouldn't understand what that feels like, would you?'

Joe sighed. 'I'm Irish, Jess. Of course I understand what that feels like.'

Now that I'd started crying, I didn't seem to be able to stop. Joe pulled me gently into his arms, and I sobbed against his shoulder. After a moment or two, my ams crept round his waist, and I held him tightly.

'Jesminder!'

I nearly jumped out of my skin. Oh my God, it was Dad.

ELEVEN

We drove home in complete silence. A tense, embarrassed silence that you could have cut with a knife. Dad didn't say a word, but I could see his hands gripping the steering wheel grimly as if he was hanging on for dear life.

I sat in the passenger seat, going hot and cold all over as I thought about what had happened. My dad had caught me wrapped in the arms of my *gora* coach when I was supposed to be dying of flu at home. I was so embarrassed, I didn't even have the words to describe how I felt. If I could have dug a big hole and buried myself in it, I would have.

I didn't understand how Dad had found out where I was. Why wasn't he at the temple like he was supposed to be? Had Pinky given the game away? I'd have to get it all out of her when we got home. Still, how Dad had found out was the least of my worries. The point was he *had*.

Feeling totally depressed and ashamed, I wondered if Dad would ever speak to me again. We'd always had a pretty good relationship, although Mum said he spoiled me. And talking of Mum, was Dad going to tell her? I groaned at the thought of all the extra grief I was going to get. I'd probably be grounded until I'd left university at this rate.

We arrived home, and Dad parked the car in silence. He said nothing to me as we climbed out and walked over to the front door. I was completely unnerved, and didn't know if I should say something first. But what *could* I say? 'By the way, I lied to you again so that I could play football, and I'm also in love with my coach, who you saw me hugging'? I think Dad knew most of that, without me having to spell it out.

As we went inside, I heard the murmur of Punjabi from the living-room. I was shocked to see that Teetu and his revolting parents were there, talking to Mum. Pinky was sitting halfway up the stairs wearing one of her best suits and made-up to within an inch of her life. She grinned and beckoned to me as we went in.

'Oh, here he is,' Mum beamed, as she spotted Dad. I braced myself for a million questions about where I'd been when I was supposed to be sick, but Mum barely noticed me. 'Tejinder's parents have come to speak to us about the wedding.'

I hurried up the stairs towards Pinky. 'What's happening?'

'Teetu's mum and dad have come to eat dirt,' Pinky whispered, smiling all over her face. 'Stupid cow, I don't know who she thinks she is in that sari.'

'No mother can stand by and see her son go through this,' Teetu's mother said melodramatically. She seemed to have forgotten that it was *her* fault that the wedding was called off in the first place. 'Teetu has been devastated.'

'Well, our Pinky, she didn't come out of her room for days,' my mum chimed in.

'Teetu also,' his mum shot back. 'For days he has eaten nothing.'

'Our children's happiness should come first,' Teetu's dad added.

It was beginning to look as if the wedding was definitely back on, then. Pinky beamed happily at me, and I forced a smile. I was glad something was going right for somebody.

Teetu's parents were all sweetness and light as they said goodbye – a bit different from the last time they'd set foot in our house. Pinky, Mum and Dad went outside to see them off, while I moped listlessly round the living-room. I wished Dad would tell Mum and get it over with. I wanted to know what my punishment was going to be.

A sudden thought struck me. I wondered how long Dad had been at the ground. Maybe he'd actually seen me play? Or score a goal? Maybe he'd been impressed by my skills – or just disgusted at my sending off . . . The brief excitement that had flared up inside me died away. As far as my parents were concerned, I was going to be a lawyer, and that was that. My exam results would be arriving in the next few days, and I was almost beginning to wish that I'd fail. I couldn't be a lawyer if I didn't get good grades.

Pinky whirled back into the room, looking like she'd just won the lottery.

'I'm getting married!' she announced, hugging Mum and then me. I glanced over at Dad, trying to catch his eye. I was sort of hoping that he might have softened a bit now that we had some good news. But he still wouldn't meet my gaze.

'We'll give them a wedding party they won't forget their whole lives!' Mum announced firmly. 'We must find out which date the hall is free again.'

Dad went over to the phone.

'Jessie, get the old wedding cards,' Mum went on. 'They're in the extension. We can change the date by hand.'

I went to get the box of invitations. When I came back, Dad was talking into the phone, asking about possible dates for the reception.

'We'll have chicken, lamb and paneer tikka as well,' Mum was boasting. 'We'll show them we're not poor!'

Dad covered the mouthpiece with one hand, and looked at Mum and Pinky. 'Will Sunday the 25th be OK?' he asked.

'The 25th?' I repeated, my insides flipping over. The 25th was the day of the final against QPR.

'No, that's too soon,' Mum hissed, much to my relief. 'We need more time.'

Dad shook his head. 'The 25th is the only available date,' he said. 'After that, there's nothing for five months.'

'Oh, *please*, don't make me wait that long,' Pinky wailed anxiously.

'But, Dad—' I began. I could see my chances of playing in the final going even further down the drain than they already were.

'Quiet!' Dad said sternly. 'Your sister needs you.'

I swallowed hard. Mum and Pinky were too busy looking at the invitations and discussing the wedding food to notice that I was trying desperately to stop myself from crying. I'd promised myself that the final would be my very last game. Even if I had to lie and cheat my way out of the house on the 25th, I'd decided that I was going to do it. After all, it was only one day out of the rest of my life, and from then on I was going to do what my parents wanted. But now it had all been taken out of my hands. There was no way I could miss my sister's wedding.

It was the day before the wedding, and Dad was putting the fairy lights back up on the front of the house. I was helping him by holding the ladder steady. We still weren't speaking, although I was relieved that Dad didn't seem to have said anything to Mum, and she and Pinky were too hassled by all the wedding preparations to notice that anything was wrong.

Still holding the ladder, I was daydreaming about the final I wouldn't be playing in, when I suddenly got a big shock. Jules was walking down the street towards me, an embarrassed look on her face.

'Jess,' she called.

I stared at her. 'Hi,' I gulped.

'I need to talk to you,' Jules muttered, looking as if having to talk to me was worse than having all her teeth pulled out.

I nodded, and looked up at Dad. He must have recognised Jules from the team, but he didn't say anything as I led her inside. Mum and Pinky were in the kitchen, arguing about the food for the reception, and they were making so much noise they didn't hear us going upstairs.

I took Jules into my bedroom, and closed the door. She glanced round at my Beckham posters, then sat down at my desk. I looked at her curiously as I plonked myself down on the bed. I was dying to know why she was here when she'd barely said two words to me recently.

There was silence for a moment.

'We all missed you at training today,' Jules said eventually. 'Especially Joe.' We both blushed. 'He told me what happened with your dad.'

'He did?' I was surprised. It looked as if Joe and Jules had sorted things out between them, then. I wondered how that had come about.

'Yeah, he's worried that he's got you into even more trouble,' Jules went on, sounding concerned herself, which was the last thing I expected.

'I'm really in the shit,' I burst out. 'My dad hasn't talked to me since. He'll never let me go back to Joe and the team.'

Jules looked at me pleadingly. 'But you *can't* miss the final, Jess! Joe told me there's going to be an American scout there. He's already watched us play in Germany, but I didn't know that until Joe told me this morning.'

So *that* was why Jules had forgiven Joe, I thought. She was concentrating on the scout and what it might mean for her footballing career.

'I can't play,' I said dully. Jules was talking about her own future here, not mine. Mine was already decided. 'It's the same day as my sister's wedding.'

For once, Jules didn't have a quick answer. 'Well, can't you get away for a *bit*?' she asked at last.

I shook my head. 'You don't understand . . .' I'd have to give her a lesson in Indian culture for her to realise that what she was asking me to do was unthinkable.

'You're giving up football now,' Jules said sharply. 'What are you going to have to give up next?'

'Oh, don't rub it in!' I retorted, stung. She'd hurt me, and now I wanted to hurt her back. 'You only came here 'cos you need me if that scout shows up!'

Jules jumped up, looking wounded, and I felt terrible. 'Look, I came here because Joe was worried about you,' she snapped, pulling the door open. 'I'll just tell him he's wasting his bloody time, shall I?'

She clattered off down the stairs before I could reply, and I heard the front door slam behind her. I lay down on the bed, and buried my head in the pillow. I hadn't meant to hurt Jules, but the truth was – I was jealous. Everything was working out for her, and nothing was going right for me. My exam results were due tomorrow morning, and if I got my A-level grades, then I was off to Kingston Uni to become a lawyer. My life was unfolding in front of me, and I had no say in the matter. None at all.

'Hurry *up*, Mum,' I said impatiently.

I was standing there in my dressing-gown, while Mum was praying in front of the picture of Guru Nanak, my results envelope in her hand. I hadn't had a chance to open it yet. Dad was waiting to find out my results too, and he was already late for work.

Mum handed me the envelope, and I tore it open. Half of me was hoping that I'd failed, which would solve the problem of having to become a lawyer. But when I focused on the results, I saw numbly that I'd got what I needed. Two As and a B.

Silently I passed the letter to Dad. His face lit up when he saw it, and he looked proud of me for the first time in days. That didn't make me feel any better though.

'Good.' He gave the letter to Mum, who was beaming and thanking Guru Nanak. 'Now you'll be a fine, top-class solicitor.'

I nodded and turned away. I saw Mum and Dad look at each other, as if they couldn't understand why I was so down. I couldn't tell them that it felt like I'd signed my own death warrant.

I trailed upstairs to get dressed. After that, I started taking my Beckham posters off my bedroom walls. Mum had reminded me that Biji would be staying in my room for the wedding, and she didn't want to look at pictures of a shaven-headed man. I took the posters down carefully, although I didn't know if I'd be putting them back up again. What was the point? I ought to start putting up posters of famous lawyers now . . .

I glanced out into the back garden at the row of brightly coloured shalwar kameez fluttering on the washing-line. Yesterday, after I'd hung out the washing, I'd practised bending a ball round it. I'd done it too, the best Beckham-like shot I'd ever managed. Thanks to Joe's coaching, I'd become better at football than I'd ever dreamed of. But it was all for nothing. *Don't think about Joe*, I told myself, *it hurts too much* . . .

Later that day, the house began to fill up with our relatives, and everybody gathered in the back garden for the *vatna* ceremony. Pinky was glowing and happy in a new green suit, enjoying being the centre of attention as she sat in the middle of everyone. The women spread the *vatna* paste – turmeric or something – on Pinky's face and arms. Kind of a purification thing. I heard Meena and Bubbly muttering that it would take more than that to make Pinky pure. They could talk!

Anyway, we were all sitting there when Dad came outside with Biji, who'd just arrived. I hadn't seen her for years because she lived in Nairobi, and I'd forgotten how incredibly old she was. I think she'd forgotten too, because she was wearing bright red lipstick and loads of gold jewellery and dressed like she was about thirty-five instead of eighty-five.

Her grandson was with her, carrying their cases. I suppose he was OK looking. Monica, Bubbly and

Meena certainly thought so. They were checking him out big-time, and Bubbly's tongue was virtually down to her knees. I didn't really take a lot of notice of him – until I saw that he seemed to be watching *me*. Whenever I looked round, he was staring, and once he even *winked*. I glared at him, and kept out of his way after that. I didn't want anyone getting any ideas.

That evening, all the women were busy making food for the reception the next day. The garden was still full of people. Most of the men (including Biji's grandson, thank God) had gone inside to drink whisky, but Dad was deep-frying *jalebis* on the outside cooker, and there was a long assembly line of aunties making samosas. I'd managed to escape so far. I was dribbling a ball around the lawn, dreaming of scoring the winning goal in the final tomorrow, even though I wouldn't be playing – when Mum pounced.

'Jesminder, do I have to die before you offer to help us?' she snapped. 'Go and give your aunties a hand with the samosas.'

Gloomily, I joined the end of the line. My job was to pinch the two triangles of pastry together to seal them after they'd been filled. Meanwhile, the aunties chattered on, ignoring me. As I sealed my fifteenth samosa, I thought I might just scream with boredom if something didn't happen soon.

It did, although it wasn't quite what I was expecting. We'd all moved inside, into the living-room, and Biji was dancing around, holding the *jaggo* on her head. It's a kind of brass pot covered in lighted candles, a bit of a fire hazard really. Dad told me that back home in India, the bride's relatives would sing and dance their way through the village with the *jaggo* the night before the wedding. Lucky we didn't have to dance round Hounslow with it – we'd probably have been arrested.

Biji put the *jaggo* on my head and everyone cheered and applauded. I began to spin round slowly in a circle, holding the pot and trying to stop it setting my hair on fire.

'She's next in line,' I heard someone say gleefully.

'Biji's grandson is a nice boy,' someone else replied.

Suddenly I felt dizzy and hot. An auntie took the pot off my head, and I stumbled out of the room, avoiding Biji's grandson who was standing near the door. I needed some fresh air.

I headed towards the front door and froze. Dad

was in the doorway, watching Joe walk off down our drive.

'Dad!' I gulped, rushing over to him. 'What did he say?'

Dad looked at me sternly. 'Don't play with your future, *beti*,' he warned me, and walked away.

I could have let it go, but I didn't. I ran straight out of the house after Joe.

'Wait!'

Joe turned round, looking surprised but pleased.

'I'm sorry about the final,' I told him.

'No, *I'm* sorry, Jess,' Joe said gently.

'I got my results,' I explained. 'I'll be starting university soon. So I won't have time for training and stuff.' My voice sounded pathetically feeble, as if I was trying to convince myself.

'That's a shame,' Joe said bluntly. 'I could've seen you playing for England some day. Jules still has a shot.'

'She told me about the scout coming,' I mumbled, wishing I didn't feel so jealous. 'I'm sorry I'm letting her down.' I don't know why I didn't just tattoo *I'm sorry* on my forehead. It was all I seemed to be saying these days.

'I asked that scout to come for you too,' Joe went

on. 'He's interested in *both* of you. That's what I was just telling your dad.'

'He's interested in *me*?' I gasped. Suddenly a whole, tempting new world was opening up again – and it didn't involve Kingston University and becoming a solicitor. 'Why are you doing this to me, Joe?' I looked up at him sadly. 'Every time I talk myself out of it, you come around and make it sound so easy.'

'I guess I don't want to give up on you,' Joe admitted quietly.

We stood there in silence. In the background we could hear loud singing coming from the house, as if to remind me where I belonged.

'So, are you promised to one of those blokes in there?' Joe asked, trying to sound casual.

'No, don't be silly.' I blushed bright red and stared down at my shoes. I couldn't look at him. 'I'm not promised to anyone.'

'You're lucky to have a family that cares so much about you,' Joe said. 'Go on, you'd better get back. Hope it all goes well for your sister tomorrow, and good luck with your studies.' I realised with a shock that he was saying goodbye. 'Come and see us sometime.'

I watched him get into his car and drive off. There was nothing more to say. I'd made my decision – or rather, I'd had it made for me.

I dragged myself back inside, trying to put on a cheerful smile even though I felt nauseous. A loud bhangra track was playing and everybody was up on their feet, dancing, even Mum and Dad. I gritted my teeth as Biji's grandson grabbed my hand and pulled me over to dance with him. I put up with it for a couple of minutes, but then he picked me up in his arms and whirled round the room with me. I felt like punching him. Everyone was watching and pointing and nudging each other. I didn't want to know what the aunties were saying about us, but I could guess.

I wriggled out of his grasp, and headed for the door. He looked a bit annoyed, but when he turned round Bubbly was standing there, ready to jump in and take my place, so he soon cheered up.

I stood in the doorway, feeling suddenly alone in the middle of all those people. This was going to be *my* life too. University, a solicitor's job, marriage to someone like Biji's grandson, kids . . .

I couldn't see any way out. I was trapped.

TWELVE

A cheer went up from the guests standing outside the house, as Pinky stepped through the front door. She looked like the perfect, shy, Indian bride, all dressed up in red and gold. I followed her, trying to stay in the background, although that wasn't easy in my bright pink sari. One of our cousins was videoing the wedding, and I was determined to stay out of his way as much as I could.

'Eyes down, don't smile,' he called, pointing the camera at Pinky. 'An Indian bride never smiles – you'll ruin the video!'

But Pinky couldn't help smiling, even though an Indian bride is supposed to look sad because she's leaving her family. She'd got what she wanted, and I could tell she was going to enjoy every minute of it.

'Where's the flippin' Rolls?' Pinky scowled, suddenly forgetting her shy bride act as she looked up and down the street for the wedding car. 'Can't any flippin' thing happen without me sorting it out?'

Luckily, the car turned up a few minutes later,

Pinky resumed her serene expression and we all set off for the ceremony at the temple.

When we arrived, we waited outside for Teetu and his family. He turned up on a white horse, which was the traditional way for the bridegroom to arrive – although it was probably a lot easier to organise back home in India than it was in Hounslow.

A white couple walked past, staring at us as if we were all mad. Teets *did* look pretty nervous – I don't think he'd ever been on a horse before. Or maybe he was just worried that his mum and sister dancing alongside the horse would scare it. But it seemed quite calm, flicking its mane and trotting mildly along the high street, oblivious to the traffic inching past.

At last we filed into the temple, taking it in turns to bow to the Guru Granth Sahib, the holy book. I glanced at my watch. Only a couple of hours to kick-off. The girls would all be at the ground by now, and Joe would be giving them a pre-game pep talk. I wanted to be there with them so much. I noticed Dad looking at me, and quickly fixed a bright smile to my face. My jaw already ached with the effort of trying to look happy all the time, and the day wasn't even half over yet. I sat through the prayers and the singing, trying to keep my mind on what was happening. As Teetu and Pinky got up to walk round the Guru Granth Sahib four times, I tried to picture myself in her position. Maybe one day. In about twenty years' time . . .

After the ceremony, we came out into the sunshine, and showered the newly-weds with petals and confetti. Great day for the match, I thought, looking up at the blue sky. *Stop it, Jess. Just stop it.*

Tony, who was standing next to me, gave me a concerned look. 'You all right about missing the final, Jess?' he asked.

I glanced over at my parents. They were watching Pinky and Teetu, and smiling proudly. I hadn't seen them look so happy for ages. I turned to Tony and nodded. What else could I do?

At the reception hall, everyone got stuck into the free cocktails and snacks, while they waited for the meal to be served. There was a bhangra band coming on later, and the party would probably go on into the night. I glanced at my watch again. It was almost time for kick-off.

Suddenly, Tony appeared beside me. He grabbed my arm and hustled me out of the hall and down a long corridor. The caterers were going up and down the corridor wheeling huge pots and platters of food into the hall, and I had to lift up my sari with one hand to dodge around them.

'Tony!' I gasped, when we finally came to a standstill. 'What are you *doing*?'

'You can still make the kick-off if we leave now,' Tony said in a determined voice.

I stared at him as if he was mad. He *was* mad. 'My mum and dad'll go spare!' I pointed out. 'You know I've got to put them first today.'

'But, Jess, there's so many people in there, they won't even notice,' Tony argued.

For a moment I wavered. But however much I wanted to, I just couldn't do it. 'I can't,' I said, my voice shaking. 'Look how happy they are, Tony. I don't want to ruin it for them.'

'What are you going to ruin?'

I almost jumped out of my sari. Dad had come up behind us, and neither Tony nor I had seen him.

'Nothing,' I said firmly, shooting Tony a warning glance. 'It's OK.'

He ignored me. 'It's the final of her football tournament. We can pick up her kit, and I can drive her there and back. It won't take long—'

'Stop it, Tony,' I broke in. 'Dad, it doesn't matter.

This is much more important. I don't want to spoil the day for you and Mum.'

Dad looked at me steadily. 'Pinky is so happy today,' he said abruptly. 'And you, you look like you're at your father's funeral.'

I hung my head. 'I'm sorry, Dad.'

'If this is the only way I'm going to see you smiling on your sister's wedding day, then go.' I jerked my head up, hardly able to believe my ears. 'But when you come back, I want to see you happy on the video.'

This time the big smile on my face was for real. I threw my arms round Dad and hugged him tightly.

'Play well, and make us proud,' he whispered in my ear.

The game would have already started by the time we got there, but I wouldn't have missed much. Tony took me home to grab my kit, and then drove as fast as the speed limit would let him towards the ground. Meanwhile, I was in the back seat, unwrapping my sari to save time. I wriggled into my kit and kicked off Mrs Paxton's shoes with the diamante bows. As I laced up my boots, Tony spun into the car park and ground to a screeching halt.

I leapt out of the car, and ran towards the pitch.

My adrenaline was rocketing as I pushed my way through the crowd and vaulted over the barrier, rushing over to Joe who was standing shouting on the touchline. His face broke into a huge smile when he saw me, but he didn't stop to ask any questions.

'Start warming up, Bhamra,' he said, giving my shoulder a squeeze. 'We're one-nil down.'

One-nil down. That was a bit of a shock. Still, there was plenty of time for us to come back. We were only about twenty minutes into the first half.

I did my stretches, then jogged impatiently on the touchline, waiting for my chance to get on to the pitch. It came when Mel fouled one of the other team, and they got a free kick. I dashed on to the field as a sub, getting patted on the back and cheered by the other Harriers as I passed. Jules had only just noticed me, and her mouth dropped open in amazement.

'I'm so glad you came!' she yelled, giving me a huge hug. Relief surged through me. It was going to be OK.

Together, we lined up alongside the others to make a defensive wall, as one of the QPR players placed the ball for their free kick. They were only just outside the penalty area, and this was their chance to grab another goal. I could feel the blood rushing in my ears as I watched the player run up to take it. Being two down would be no joke. But the ball sailed over the top of the wall, and Charlie caught it safely.

Now that Jules and I were back in business as friends *and* team-mates, we played better than ever. Our passes were fast and sharp and accurate, and we moved smoothly down the pitch, almost reading each other's minds as the ball flew between us. We were ripping the heart out of the QPR defence. It was only a matter of time before we scored.

I watched as Mel passed the ball to Jules while we ran from the centre into the QPR half. I knew what Jules was going to do – and she did it. She let the ball roll through her legs to me, completely fooling the QPR defence. I picked it up quickly behind her, allowing Jules to run forward nearer to the goal, then I threaded a neat pass towards her. Jules was on to it in a flash, and a second later the ball was sitting in the corner of the net.

Jules screamed 'YES!' and ran round the pitch with her top over her head, showing off her sports bra. I couldn't stop laughing. Joe was going mad on the touchline, while the rest of us jumped on top of Jules, hugging her to death.

QPR weren't about to give up, though. They fought hard, and there were several near misses. The second half was just as close. By the eighty-fifth minute, I was beginning to think that we'd be playing extra time to decide the tournament winners. But, as it happened, I was wrong.

Jules slotted the ball through to me, and I set off at a run, weaving in and out of the QPR defenders, who were getting tired. I was on the edge of the box when I suddenly felt my ankles chopped from underneath me.

'Ow!' I yelped, tumbling over on to the grass as the ref blew his whistle.

One of the defenders had floored me with a late tackle. Now we had a free kick, right on the edge of the box. The perfect place for a Beckham special.

Jules grinned at me. 'It's yours, Jess,' she said.

The ref was pointing at the spot where the ball had to go. I placed it carefully, then took a few steps backwards. I took a deep breath and looked down at the ball, then up at the QPR wall.

But in my mind, the QPR players had vanished. Instead there stood Mum, three old aunties and Pinky in her wedding suit. They were all shaking their heads at me and looking disapproving.

But I wasn't going to let them put me off. I blinked a few times, and they disappeared. *This was it*.

I took a short run, and hit the edge of the ball with my inside right foot. It flew exactly where I wanted it to go, which was round the side of the wall without being deflected by any of the QPR players. Then it curved sweetly past the goalie. She flung herself sideways in a vain attempt to reach it, but it dipped over her head and into the net just below the crossbar. I could hardly believe it.

I'd bent it just like Beckham. It was my best shot *ever*.

'We won the cup! We won the cup!'

The match was over, and the Harriers were the summer tournament champions. We were back in the changing-room, after doing several victory laps round the pitch with the cup, and everyone was singing and laughing and cheering. I was joining in, but I was also trying to get out of my kit and put my sari on at the same time. I had to get back to the wedding before anyone missed me.

'We'll help you!' Jules offered, giggling, and she and the other girls began wrapping me up in my sari as if they were doing up a parcel.

'I can't get the folds right!' I said, laughing so hard my stomach hurt. 'Stop it, I'm going to have to unwind it.'

There was a rap on the door. 'Paxton, Bhamra, are you decent?' Joe called.

Jules grabbed my arm, and we rushed outside, me tucking in my sari as I went. Joe and a short, stocky guy in a baseball cap were waiting outside. The American scout.

Jules clutched my hand as the guy talked to us. We were great, he said, we'd really impressed him. He wanted to recommend us both for scholarships to Santa Clara college, who had one of the top teams. It wouldn't cost us anything. We could be professionals, with the chance to make loads of money . . .

I was so excited, my mind was spinning. I couldn't think straight. My dreams were being handed to me on a plate, and all I had to do was grab them. I glanced at Joe to see if he looked happy for us. He was smiling, but his eyes were sad. I suddenly felt cold at the thought of going to America, and leaving him behind. But this was my future we were talking about . . .

When Joe took the scout off to the bar to buy him

a drink, I flung my arms round Jules and kissed her, completely overwhelmed with excitement.

'I can't believe it!' I gasped. '*Both* of us!'

'Yeah, that's what makes it so brilliant.' Jules hugged me back, her eyes shining.

As we drew apart, I noticed that Jules' mum and dad were waiting for her a short distance away. In her big pink straw hat and flowery dress, Mrs Paxton looked like she was ready for a day at the races rather than the football. Still, it was nice of her to come. Maybe she was getting used to the idea of Jules playing at last. But, come to think of it, she wasn't looking too happy. She was staring at me and Jules in dismay. I wondered what was the matter. Maybe she was just sad because she'd guessed Jules was on her way to the States.

'Look, come over to my sister's wedding reception when you've changed, yeah?' I said, turning to Jules. 'We can celebrate properly there.'

'OK, that'd be great.' Jules looked thrilled to be invited.

I ran off to find Tony. Though I should have been exhausted after the game, I was buzzing. When I told him about America, Tony was as excited as I was, and we talked about nothing else the whole way back to the reception. When we got there, the party was in full swing. The bhangra band was playing and everyone was dancing – there'd even been a fight: between Biji's grandson and the cameraman. Apparently the cameraman had filmed Biji's grandson snogging Bubbly in the women's loos.

No-one seemed to have missed me, although Mum gave me a funny look when I ran up to Dad and gave him a big hug.

'We won,' I whispered, beaming all over my face.

He nodded, but didn't say anything. I was swept up in the circle of dancers and, as I moved away, I noticed Tony dancing near a really good-looking Indian boy who was smiling at him! I grinned to myself. Maybe there were happy endings round the corner for both of us . . .

At last it was time for the *Doli* ceremony, and we all went outside. The *Doli* is when the bride officially leaves her own family and joins her husband's, and it's always really sad. Pinky was hugging Mum and crying into a tissue, and I was even beginning to feel tearful too, when a car suddenly swept up the drive and stopped abruptly in front of us. It was Jules and her mum. I waved at them. Jules waved back, but her mum glared at me through the car window. God, what *was* the matter with the woman?

Suddenly Mrs Paxton got out of the car and marched over to me, giving me a filthy look. I took a step backwards, wondering what on earth was going on. Everyone, including Pinky, stopped crying and waited to see what would happen.

Mrs Paxton stared me straight in the eye. 'How *could* you be such a hypocrite?' she demanded in a tearful voice.

I looked at her nervously. I didn't have a clue what she was on about.

'Mum!' hissed Jules, hovering in the background.

'How could you be here all respectful with your lot –' Mrs Paxton glanced at my assembled relatives who were all watching goggle-eyed to see what this mad *gori* would do next '– when I *know* you've been kissing my daughter in broad daylight?'

I gasped, and Jules turned bright red. For God's sake. I'd kissed Jules earlier – but we were only celebrating! She was acting like we'd had a full-on snog or something.

Mrs Paxton looked down at my feet and did a double-take. For a moment I didn't understand why, but then I remembered. The shoes with diamante bows. *Her* shoes.

'Get your lesbian feet out of my shoes!' she snapped.

Lesbian? I nearly dropped dead on the spot. Mrs Paxton thought Jules and I were *lesbians*? No wonder she'd been acting all upset.

'Lesbian?' I heard Biji say in a puzzled voice. 'Her birthday's in March. I thought she was a Pisces.'

'She's not Lebanese, she's Punjabi,' Tony's mum added helpfully.

Pinky pushed her way forward and stared aggressively at Mrs Paxton. 'Do you mind?' she snapped. 'This happens to be my wedding day.'

I didn't know whether to laugh or cry. I slipped my feet out of the shoes, and handed them to Mrs Paxton. Jules immediately grabbed her mum's elbow and hustled her over to the car, looking as if she was ready to kill her. Meanwhile, all the relatives stood around, looking unsure about what to do next. Then some of them remembered that it was supposed to be the *Doli* ceremony, and they all started wailing and crying again. Covering her face with her sari, Pinky climbed into the car and pulled me in with her.

'What the bleeding hell's going on?' she demanded, her tears drying up like magic. 'What was that *gori* on about you being a lez? I thought you fancied your coach.'

'I don't know what she meant,' I replied. Mrs Paxton was the least of my worries – anyway, Jules would soon put her mother straight.

'Jess.' Pinky leaned towards me. 'Don't you want all this?' she asked urgently, gesturing at her wedding sari and gold jewellery. 'It's the best day of your life!'

'I want *more* than this,' I said quietly. 'They've offered me and Jules a scholarship to go to America.'

'What?' Pinky was shocked. 'Jess, there's no way Dad'll let you go and live abroad without getting married first!'

My dreams cracked and crumbled into dust around me. She was right. I'd been so happy that Dad had let me play today, I'd refused to face the truth. Giving me permission to play in the final had been a giant step for Dad. But asking him if I could go to university in the States and play for a US team?

It just wasn't going to happen.

But surely I couldn't give up my whole future without *trying* to persuade them . . . could I?

THIRTEEN

The wedding was over. Pinky had gone, and the house seemed quiet and empty without her. Mum, Dad, Biji and Tony's parents were sitting in the living-room, talking over everything that had happened at the wedding, while I made tea in the kitchen. Tony was helping me. He looked worried as I carried the tray into the living-room and handed round the cups. I knew what was on his mind, because it was the same thing that was on mine.

'I didn't understand what that English woman was talking about,' Biji complained, as she took her tea. 'What was she saying about kissing?'

'I think she got confused, like Teetu's parents,' Mum yawned. 'It's so hard when young people have such short hair.'

'English people always complain when we have our functions,' Tony's mum added. 'But why did she take Jesminder's shoes?'

I slipped away before someone could ask me about Mrs Paxton again, and went back to Tony.

'How am I gonna tell them, Tony?' I muttered. 'I

have to, or I'll end up a solicitor, bored out of my mind.'

Tony frowned. I wasn't really expecting him to come up with any ideas – after all, this was *my* problem, not his – but suddenly he grabbed my hand and pulled me into the living-room.

'Mum, Dad, Uncleji, Auntieji,' Tony announced, standing in front of the sofa with me at his side. 'We've got something to tell you.'

Oh no, I thought. *Tony, what are you doing?* I didn't have a clue what he was up to, but all the adults were sitting up now, their ears practically flapping.

'You know how we've been good friends for a long time . . .' Tony started.

Oh, God, I thought, as everyone sat forward eagerly in their seats.

'Well, we'd like to ask for your blessings,' Tony said awkwardly. 'We want to get engaged!'

I stared at him in shock. Meanwhile Tony's mum clasped her hands and started blessing us immediately, and there were exclamations of delight from the others. I just stood there dumbly, not knowing what to say. What the hell was Tony up to? If he wanted to marry me, he might have discussed it with me first.

'There's just one condition.' Tony had to raise his voice to be heard above all the rejoicing. 'I want Jesminder to go to college first, anywhere she wants.'

I felt all the colour drain from my face and I clutched Tony's hand, unable to speak. He'd worked out a way for me to go to America, and this was it. Mum and Dad were much more likely to let me go if I was already engaged to a nice Sikh boy they approved of. It was a brilliant idea.

'Of course, son,' Dad agreed eagerly. 'That's what I want too.'

I bit my lip. I couldn't *believe* that Tony was prepared to do this for me. He was a real friend. But if we went through with this fake engagement, I'd be lying to my parents *again*. Tony and I would never be getting married, which meant we'd have to split up at some point and tell our parents the reason why. And what about the future? After university, I might want to stay in America for a while. Or what if I came back to Britain and had to start driving a cab like that girl in the England team, just so I could carry on playing football? That would mean more painful arguments as I carried on fighting to live my life the way I wanted to. Quickly I made up my mind. No more secrets, no more lies.

'Mum, Dad, Tony's lying,' I blurted out. 'We're not getting married.'

Everyone stopped celebrating, and looked confused.

'Tony only said that to help me,' I went on shakily. 'Look, I played in the final today – and we won.'

'What?' Mum asked in a shocked voice. 'How?'

'I wasn't going to go, but Dad let me,' I told her.

For once, Mum was too stunned to say a word. She turned to Dad, who looked bit shamefaced.

'And it was brilliant,' I went on quickly before Mum could get started. 'I played the best I ever have – because I wasn't sneaking off and lying to you. I didn't *ask* to be good at football –' I glanced at the picture on the wall '– Guru Nanak must have blessed me. Anyway, there was a scout from America there who's offered me a place at a top university with a free scholarship and a chance to play football professionally. I *really* want to go . . .' I was having to swallow hard now because I was on the edge of tears. 'And if I can't tell you now what I really want, then I'll never be happy *whatever* I do.'

I stole a glance at Mum and Dad. Dad look stunned, but Mum was recovering fast. She glared at Dad. 'You mean you let her leave her sister's wedding to play *football*?'

Tears filled my eyes, and I slumped down in an armchair. Hadn't Mum heard a word I'd been saying?

'You might have been able to handle her long face, but I couldn't,' Dad muttered uncomfortably. 'I didn't have the heart to stop her.'

'And *that's* why she's ready to go all the way to America now!' Mum snapped.

I huddled in my chair, feeling sick. I'd blown it. I'd really blown it.

There was a tense silence. Dad got up, went over to the bar in the corner and poured himself a large whisky.

'When those bloody English cricket players threw me out of their club like a dog, I never complained,' he said quietly. 'On the contrary, I vowed never to play again. And who suffered? Me.'

I stared at him. Of all the things I'd expected him to say, this wasn't one of them.

'I don't want Jessie to suffer,' Dad said. 'I don't want her to make the same mistake her father made, just accepting the situation. I want her to fight, and I want her to win.'

I sat up, my eyes fixed on him. A tiny seed of hope sprang up inside me and started to grow.

'I've seen Jessie play, and she's brilliant!' Dad went on passionately. I managed a smile. So he *had* seen me playing in the semi-final. 'I don't think anyone has the right to stop her . . .'

I gasped with relief, jumped up from my chair and ran to throw my arms round him. Mum might talk a lot, but if Dad had made up his mind about something, then that was it. I was so happy, I couldn't say a word, I just hugged him as tightly as I could.

'Two daughters made happy in one day,' Dad said softly. 'What more could any father want?'

'Well, at least I've taught her how to cook a full Indian dinner,' Mum said, sounding upset but resigned. 'The rest is in God's hands!'

'Joe! Joe!' I raced across the pitch, holding my sari up with one hand. He was out under the floodlights on his own, juggling a football on his knees. 'I'm going! They said I could go!'

At first he looked stunned, then he beamed as I threw myself into his arms and we hugged each other to bits. 'That's brilliant, Jess.'

There were a few wolf whistles from some guys on the neighbouring pitch, and I pulled away from him, embarrassed.

'Sorry, I forgot.'

'It's OK now, Jess,' Joe said quickly. 'I'm not your coach any more. We can do what we want.'

He reached out to pull me to him again, but I backed away. This was one of the hardest things I'd ever had to do. But I'd thought things through, and it was the only way.

'Joe,' I began uncomfortably.

Joe looked behind him, an expression of alarm on his face. 'Your dad's not here, is he?'

I shook my head. 'I'm sorry, Joe. I can't . . .'

Joe looked confused and I almost melted, but I forced myself to harden my heart again. 'Jess, I thought you wanted—'

'Letting me go is a really big step for my mum and dad.' I couldn't look at him. Instead, I reached out and fiddled with the zip of his trackie top. 'I don't know how they'd survive if I told them about you too.'

There was silence for a moment.

'Well, I guess with you going to America, there's not much point anyway,' Joe said bravely. 'Is there?'

He was giving me a way out without making it hard for me. I shook my head, and we hugged each other goodbye. It might be the right decision, but it still hurt. Why couldn't life just be simple and straightforward?

'Make sure you keep it by your bed all the time,' Mum fussed, handing me a picture of Guru Nanak. 'And call Papu Uncle in Canada as soon as you land. At least there's some family close by.'

I grinned at Tony. I didn't like to tell Mum how far away from Canada Santa Clara actually *was*.

'*Beti*, go with our blessings,' Dad added, 'but call us every week.'

The big day had finally arrived. Jules and I were flying out to America for our first term at the university, and Tony and my parents had come to Heathrow to see me off. I was buzzing with anticipation, but it was hard to tear myself away from Mum and Dad. Our flight had already been called four times, and Jules and I were going to be the last passengers to board if we weren't careful.

Jules was standing with her parents a little way off – they were still saying their goodbyes too. I was glad that everything had been sorted out with Mrs

Paxton. Jules had told me that her mum had overheard us rowing in Jules' bedroom about Joe, and thought we were in love with each other! She must've been mad. I could laugh about it now, though. *Joe*. I shook my head to get the thought of him out of my mind. I had to look forward now.

'Excuse me.' Jules' dad came over to us. 'It's getting really late. They'd better board the plane.'

I took a deep breath as I gave Mum and Dad a final hug. This was it, then. No going back.

'Jess!'

I felt goosebumps all over me, and my face broke into a huge smile. Joe was running through the departure lounge towards me.

'What are you doing here?' I gasped, conscious of my parents' eyes on us.

'I wanted to tell you, they offered me the job,' Joe said. 'They want me to coach the men's side.'

I gave him a big smile. I wanted to hug him, but it wasn't a good idea with my parents standing there. 'That's *great*, Joe!'

'Yeah.' He nodded. 'I turned 'em down.'

'What?' My jaw dropped. 'Why—?'

'They're going to let me coach the girls' side full-time,' Joe broke in, smiling from ear to ear. 'They want us to go pro next year. Can't keep losing our best players to the Yanks now, can we?' he added teasingly.

'That's brilliant, Joe,' I said, meaning it. 'You should tell your dad.'

'I already did,' Joe replied, and the look on his face told me that everything was OK.

'Maybe after they've trained you up out there, I'll sign you back,' he went on. 'If we can afford you!'

'You wish,' I laughed.

Suddenly serious, Joe looked deep into my eyes. 'Look, Jess,' he said urgently, 'I can't let you go without knowing—'

'What?' I said. But I thought I already knew.

'That even with the distance and the concerns of your family, we might still have something . . .'

I couldn't take my eyes off him. Suddenly it was as if there was no-one else in the airport except us two. I leaned towards him, and then we were kissing. I'd forgotten about Mum and Dad standing behind us. And if I'd remembered, I wouldn't have cared anyway. I knew then that what Pinky had told me was true. *When you're in love, you'll do anything just to be with that person . . .*

'Oh my God!' It was Jules, screaming. 'It's

Beckham! Jess, look! It's Becks! It's got to be a sign . . .'

Slowly I pulled away from Joe and turned to look. Everyone was staring up at a glassed-in corridor above our heads which led to VIP passport control. None of them had even noticed us kissing. I just caught a glimpse of David and Victoria Beckham, surrounded by minders, before they disappeared from sight.

I grinned at Joe. Jules was right. It *was* a sign. 'I'm back at Christmas,' I whispered. 'We'll tackle my mum and dad then.'

The look on Joe's face gave me a warm feeling inside. He nodded, then moved over to say goodbye to Jules. There was just time for one last round of hugs before Jules and I walked towards the sliding doors.

'This is it,' Jules breathed, her eyes shining.

I turned to give my parents one last wave, and saw my mum handing a tissue to Mrs Paxton. Both of them were crying. 'Yeah, this is it,' I agreed. 'Let's go for it.'

Smiling, we turned and walked through the sliding doors. Into our future.

A note from the author

As soon as I heard about the film 'Bend it like Beckham', I wanted to write the book. I wanted to do it even more after seeing a rough cut of the film, and reading Gurinder's, Guljit's and Paul's script. Jess's story is so fresh and funny, yet it works on several different levels. At its most serious, it mirrors the struggle many young Asians face, trying to live their lives caught between two cultures. But it's also a very personal story about one girl's determination to follow her dream. I grew up in almost exactly the same kind of circumstances as Jess, and I spent most of the film nudging my husband and whispering 'That happened to me too!' But the best thing about 'Bend it Like Beckham' is that you don't have to be Asian or even a football fan to enjoy it. It's a funny, original and inspiring story for everyone.

BLUE

Sue Mayfield

'You've lost weight . . . Mind you don't get anorexic,' Hayley said, sounding concerned. 'You're all skin and bone!' She glanced sideways at Ruth Smith, and they smiled conspiratorially.

'Anna-rexic!' said Ruth with a snort of laughter . . .

When Hayley, the most popular girl at school, wants to be her best mate, new girl Anna Goldsmith can't believe her luck. But Hayley's friendship comes at a price. She enjoys playing games. Spiteful, cruel and vicious games . . .

FESTIVAL

David Belbin

The Glastonbury Festival. Three days in June. For many, it's the event of the summer – for three Glastonbury virgins and one fourteen-year-old veteran, it's going to be a life-changing experience.

Leila, exams over, just wants to have fun. But first she has to find a way to get there . . .

Jake is playing the festival. This could be his big break. Or his biggest nightmare . . .

Wilf is forced to sell his ticket, so his only way in is to jump the fence. And there's a big surprise waiting on the other side . . .

Holly gets in free. It's her tenth Glastonbury. She's promised herself it'll be the last . . .

ORDER FORM

Also available in the Bite series

0 340 80519 6	Blue *Sue Mayfield*	£4.99	❏
0 340 81732 1	Nostradamus and Instant Noodles *John Larkin*	£4.99	❏
0 340 81746 1	Festival *David Belbin*	£4.99	❏
0 340 81762 3	Speak *Laurie Halse Anderson*	£4.99	❏
0 340 80520 X	Four Days Till Friday *Pat Moon*	£4.99	❏
0 340 84148 6	Magenta Orange *Echo Freer*	£4.99	❏

All Hodder Children's books are available at your local bookshop, or can be ordered direct from the publisher. Just tick the titles you would like and complete the details below. Prices and availability are subject to change without prior notice.

Please enclose a cheque or postal order made payable to *Bookpoint Ltd*, and send to: Hodder Children's Books, 130 Milton Park, Abingdon, OXON OX14 4SB, UK. Email Address: orders@bookpoint.co.uk

If you would prefer to pay by credit card, our call centre team would be delighted to take your order by telephone. Our direct line *01235 400414* (lines open 9.00 am–6.00 pm Monday to Saturday, 24 hour message answering service). Alternatively you can send a fax on *01235 400454*.

TITLE		FIRST NAME		SURNAME	

ADDRESS	

DAYTIME TEL:		POST CODE	

If you would prefer to pay by credit card, please complete:
Please debit my Visa/Access/Diner's Card/American Express (delete as applicable) card no:

Signature .... Expiry Date: ....

If you would NOT like to receive further information on our products please tick the box. ❏